William Thomson

Leddy May

And other Poems

William Thomson

Leddy May
And other Poems

ISBN/EAN: 9783337158200

Printed in Europe, USA, Canada, Australia, Japan

Cover: Foto ©Andreas Hilbeck / pixelio.de

More available books at **www.hansebooks.com**

LEDDY MAY

AND

OTHER POEMS

BY

WILLIAM THOMSON.

"Remember, reader, it was in my youth." *Fielding.*

GLASGOW:
PUBLISHED BY T. W. FARRELL, BOOKBINDER,
136 GEORGE STREET.
1883.

TO THE

BARDIE CLAN.

GENTLEMEN,

In memory of many happy evenings spent with you since I became a member three years ago, and as a slight acknowledgment of your many kindnesses in these latter days of ill-health.

I DEDICATE THIS LITTLE BOOK TO YOU.

W. T.

ARRAN SONNETS.

Contents.

Contents.

SONNETS FROM THE FRENCH.

JUVENILIA.

THOMSON.—At 188 Holm Street, aged 22 years,
William Thomson, author of "Leddy May" and
other poems.

BALLADS.

LEDDY MAY.

I.

THE gowans glint fu' bonnilie beside the castle wa' ;
   The summer sun wi' lammer licht shines thro' the
      castle ha' ;
A leddy stan's, wi' tearfu' e'e, an' she is sabbin' sair—
"It's oh! an' oh! Lord Gregory, ye may return nae
   mair !"

"Come dry your tears an' smile again, an' listen, sweet-
   he'rt mine,
The red cross gleams upon my shield—I maun tae
   Palestine ;
But sune we'll rout the Saracens, sae, leddy, dinna grieve,
But gi'e tae me your kerchief white to wear upon my
   sleeve.

1

" 'Tae wear upon my sleeve, leddy, e'en in the battle's
     strife,
A mem'ry o' the ane I lo'e far dearer than my life ;
Betide me weal, betide me wae, I tread in duty's airt,
Tho' fause Sir Guy o' Netherlea may act the cooard's
     pairt."

She 's taen the kerchief frae her neck and bun' it roond
     his arm,
Wi' mony a prayer that Ane abune will shield him frae a'
     harm.
He clasps her han' an' kisses her, an' bravely turns awa'—
Lord Gregory has far to ride or e'er the neist day daw' !

II.

It's up the stair an' doon the stair the leddy tak's her
     way,
An' up the stair an' doon the stair a' thro' the lanesome
     day,
The wistfu' win's o' winter wail the dark fir wuds amang,
The leddy's he'rt is weary as she sings a waesome sang :

   I think on the day when my love gaed awa',
     Wi' his armour sae bricht, and his pennon sae braw,
   I try tae be blythesome an' whisper his name,
     An' think on the time when my love'll come hame ;
       But dark thochts o' evil will aftentimes stairt
       Far doon in the depths o' my he'rt, my he'rt.

The winter win's rave owre the desolate scene,
But simmer will come wi' its garment o' green ;
Tho' gin my true love comes na back owre the sea
It winna, it canna, be simmer tae me ;
 O ! win's far awa', waft his ship in the airt
 That will bring him again tae my he'rt, my he'rt.

III.

The winter's past and simmer reigns wi' croon o' flooers
  sae braw,
The gowans glint fu' bonnilie beside the castle wa',
An' frae the castle yett there rides Sir Guy o' Netherlea,
An' he has asked sweet Leddy May his lovin' bride to be.

But this was what she answered him—" Sir Guy, it canna
  be ;
My love is for Lord Gregory, my he'rt is owre the sea."
Sir Guy is forced tae turn awa', an' tak' the hameart gate:
His brow is as the sunset red, his he'rt is black wi' hate.

IV.

" O holy Palmer, tell me true, come ye frae Palestine,
An' saw ye brave Lord Gregory, wha fills this he'rt o'
  mine ?"
" Oh ! I was wi' the Christian camp upon the Eastern
  plain,
An' there I saw Lord Gregory in foremost battle slain !"

V.

"Why are ye a' sae sorrowfu', why are ye a' sae wae?"
"Yont in the castle, cauld in death, lies bonnie Leddy
  May!"
The deid-bell rings wi' solemn jowl—the stricken
  mourners kneel—
An' "Ha! ha! ha!" laughs fause Sir Guy, "*I played the
  Palmer weel!*"

VI.

"The gloamin' shadows fa', willow!
Wi' gentle gloom owre a', willow!
  An' in my he'rt love's licht
  Is mirked by sorrow's nicht—
Aneath your branches rests the ane wha made my life
  sae bricht,
  Willow!

"She was sae sweet, sae true, willow!
But I am lanely noo, willow!
  Tae leeve alane wad be
  A waefu' weird tae dree;
Ah! sune your mournfu', bendin' boughs will breathe
  their sighs owre me,
  Willow!"

Lord Gregory is kneelin' doon beside the leddy's grave,
Abune his heid the win'-blawn willow branches saftly
  wave;
The white stars skinkle brichtly as the gloamin' shadows fa',
The gowans close their waefu' e'en beside the castle wa'.

MAID MYSIE.

I.

IT'S oh! an' oh!
   That the he'rts o' men war truer!
For a lassie's love is a lassie's life,
   Tho' nocht tae a faithless wooer.

Maid Mysie gaed out wi' a beatin' he'rt
   Adoon by the birken shaw,
Tae a lanely spot whar rough-tapped firs
   Threw shadows o' gloom owre a'.

A bonnie lass wis Maid Mysie,
   Wi' smilin' e'en o' blue,
An' hair o' bricht an' sunny tint
   Abune her bonnie brent broo.

The shepherd's dochter wis Maid Mysie,
   Wha leeved on the far hillside :
An' there was ane —the laird's ae son—
   Wha socht her for his bride.

But the laird wis a pridefu' man an' stern,
   An' prood o' his ancient race,
An' sae the young laird an' Maid Mysie
   Met there in that lanesome place.

An' oh ! but she lo'ed him faithfu' an' weel,
    Wi' the love o' her youthfu' he'rt ;
But whiles when she thocht o' his faither stern,
    Wild thochts in her breist wad stairt.

" The eagle leaves na his mountain hame
    Tae mate wi' the cushie-doo ;
An' it seems sae strange for a low-born maid
    Tae wed wi' ane like you.

" An' oh," she wad cry, " will ye aye be true?
    An' oh, will ye ne'er forget ?
For if I should tine the love I ha'e won,
    Far better we ne'er had met."

But aye he kissed her, an' aye he swore
    That he lo'ed but her alane,
An' gin but the langed for time wis come
    He 'd mak' her a' his ain.

    It 's oh ! an' oh !
  That the he'rts o' men war truer !
For a lassie's love is a lassie's life
    Tho' nocht tae a faithless wooer.

        II.

Maid Mysie gaed oot wi' a beatin' he'rt
    Adoon by the birken shaw,
The win' gaed by wi' an eerie sough,
    An' nicht threw a gloom owre a'.

She waitit lang at the trystin' place,
    But the young laird cam' na there—
The time flew by on leaden wings,
    An' her he'rt grew sad an' sair.

A nicht bird uttered its lanely cry—
    A clud hid the mune's white licht—
An' aye she cooered an' asked hersel',
    " What keeps him sae late the nicht?"

Ah ! Mysie lass, he minds na you,
    Nor the charm o' yer bricht blue e'en,
But pours his passionate tale o' love
    In the ear o' Mistress Jean,

A wilfu' beauty, wi' walth o' gowd,
    An' come o' an ancient line
(The same hedge marched the twa estates—
    A bride tae his faither's min').

An' witchin' music rung thro' the ha',
    An' the lichts were burnin' bricht ;
Wi' dance an' sang an' blythesome tale
    Richt merrily passed the nicht.

An' Mysie stood wi' a burstin' he'rt
    Adoon by the birken shaw ;
The win' gaed by wi' an' eerie sough.
    An' nicht threw a gloom owre a'.

It's oh! an' oh!
'That the he'rts o' men were truer!
For a lassie's love is a lassie's life,
'Tho' nocht tae a faithless wooer.

III.

"Hush ye, hush ye, ma bonnie bairn,
The ae life-tie I ha'e;
Ye dinna ken yer mither's shame,
Nor the depth o' yer mither's wae.

"Hush ye, hush ye, ma bonnie bairn,
Oh! hoo I langed tae dee;
Yon wis a bonnie waddin', ma bairn,
But a waefu' waddin' for me.

"Oh! happy, happy bairnhood's years,
When 'twis simmer ilka day!
Bricht, bricht ye shone! but noo, alack!
Life's pleasures hae gane for aye.

"Ma mither has grown sae sad o' late,
Sae tender an' fond owre me,
An' aft when she thinks I dinna ken,
The mist comes tae her e'e.

"Ma faither's hair, ance raven black,
Is streakit enoo wi' grey,
An' his back is booed wi' heavy care,
An' I ken his he'rt is wae.

" The fowk o' the village turn awa'
  When I meet them in the lane—
Oh ! death this nicht wad be ma choice
  But for you, ma bonnie wean.

" Hush ye, hush ye, ma bonnie bairn ;
  God keep ye in Virtue's airt,
That ye mayna ken the unco stound
  That deadens yer mither's he'rt.

" Hush ye, hush ye, ma bonnie bairn,
  But for you I fain wad dee ;
Yon wis a bonnie waddin', ma bairn,
  But a waefu' waddin' for me."

    It's oh ! an oh !
  That the he'rts o' men war truer !
For a lassie's love is a lassie's life,
  Tho' nocht tae a faithless wooer.

MARJORY.

MARJORY'S garden is very fair
    (Red, red roses and lilies white),
And many a time I linger there
    (In sunny days young hearts are light).

Marjory owns both beauty and grace
    (Red, red roses and lilies white),
That is the reason I like the place
    (In sunny days young hearts are light).

Majory sits in the old green bower
    (Red, red roses and lilies white),
Laughing, she gives me my choice of a flower
    (In sunny days young hearts are light).

" You are the flower I love the best "
    (Red, red roses and lilies white);
Close to my bosom is Marjory pressed
    (In sunny days young hearts are light).

THE LAIRD O' GOWDENLEAS.

I.

THE sun glints bricht on the auld farm-house,
    An' the win' blaws saft thro' the simmer trees ;
Sweet is the sang o' the lift-hie larks,
    Blythesome the boom o' the hame-boun' bees.

At the farmer's door sits his dochter Jean
    (The win' blaws saft thro' the simmer trees),
A love-lit lowe in her bricht blue e'en,
    Her hair a' blawn wi' the playfu' breeze.

A lo'efu' lad comes liltin' by
   ('The win' blaws saft thro' the simmer trees)—
A buirdly fellow wi' curlin' hair
   An' weys a lassie's he'rt tae please.

She meets him doon at the gairden yett
   ('The win' blaws saft thro' the simmer trees);
But sadness chases the rose frae her face—
   (Love seldom travels a path o' ease).

" My faither likesna yer comin' here "
   ('The win' blaws saft thro' the simmer trees) ;
" He bade me beware o' stranger lads,
   An' heavy his word on ma puir he'rt wei's."

He kisses her lips an' he turns awa'
   ('The win' blaws saft thro' the simmer trees),
An' tears fill the e'en o' bonnie Jean
   As the auld white yett ahint him swees.

(He'rts may droop though the sun shines bricht,
   An' the win' blaws saft thro' the simmer trees ;
But joy may come when we least jalouse,
   An' Love look straught when we think he gleys.)

II.

Adoon the lane rides a gallant gay
   When the win' blaws saft through the simmer trees ;
Awa' frae his horse's soondin' staps
   The lanely maukin frichtit flees.

Adoon the lane gangs bonnie Jean
　　(The win' blaws saft thro' the simmer trees),
Trying tae quench her burnin' love,
　　But only fannin' the flichtfu' breeze.

The horseman reaches the lassie's side
　　(The win' blaws saft thro' the simmer trees),
He louts him doon frae his saddle-bow,
　　An' lifts her up wi' a canny heeze.

"Noo dinna fear ye, ma winsome Jean
　　(The win' blaws saft thro' the simmer trees),
I'll set ye doon at the gairden yett,
　　An' I will yer faither's wrath appease."

He sets her doon at the gairden yett
　　(The win' blaws saft thro' the simmer trees),
An' lichtly loups he doon tae her side—
　　Her faither glowers when the gallant he sees.

"I hae come tae ask for yer dochter's han'
　　(The win' blaws saft thro' the simmer trees),
Gowdenleas' leddy will Jeanie be,
　　For I am the Laird o' Gowdenleas!"

(He'rts may droop tho' the sun shines bricht,
　　An' the win' blaws saft thro' the simmer trees;
But joy may come when we least jalouse,
　　An' Love look straucht when we think he gleys.)

THE MAISTER AND THE BAIRNS.

THE Maister sat in a wee cot hoose
    Tae the Jordan's waters near,
An' the fisher fowk crushed an' crooded roon'
    The Maister's words tae hear.

An' even the bairns frae the near-haun' streets
    War mixin' in wi' the thrang,
Laddies an' lassies wi' wee bare feet
    Jinkin' the crood amang.

An' ane o' the Twal' at the Maister's side
    Rase up an' cried alood—
" Come, come, bairns, this is nae place for you,
    Rin awa' hame oot the crood."

But the Maister said, as they turned awa',
    " Let the wee bairns come tae me !"
An' He gaithered them roon' Him whar He sat,
    An' liftit ane up on His knee.

Ay, He gaithered them roon' Him whar He sat,
    An' straikit their curly hair,
An' He said tae the won'erin' fisher fowk
    That croodit aroon' Him there —

"Sen'na the weans awa' frae me,
  But raither this lesson learn—
That nane'll won in at heaven's yett
  That isna as pure as a bairn !"

An' He that wisna oor kith an' kin,
  But a Prince o' the Far Awa',
Gaithered the wee anes in His airms,
  An' blessed them ane an' a'.

.   .   .   .

O Thou who watchest the ways o' men
  Keep our feet in the heavenly airt,
An' bring us at last tae Thy hame abune
  As pure as the bairns in he'rt.

ALL IN THE AUTUMN GLOAMING.

IN the glow of an autumn gloaming we went wandering
    through the glade
    (Red were the berries on the rowan tree),
The breezes soft in the birchen boughs a pleasant mur-
    mur made,
And as we wandered many were the loving words we said,
    All in the autumn gloaming.

Beneath the sheltering rowan-tree we sat awhile to rest
  (Red were the berries on the rowan tree),
Still brighter grew the glories of the golden-gleaming west,
And my arm her waist encircled and her rosebud lips I
  pressed,
  All in the autumn gloaming.

I twined her a crown of rowan-leaves with berries bright
  between
  (Red were the berries on the rowan tree),
I placed it around her lily brow, 'mid her hair of golden
  sheen—
Fondly I clasped her in my arms and murmured soft,
  " My Queen !"
  All in the autumn gloaming.

Ah me! that golden autumn eve and all its dreams have
  flown
  (Red were the berries on the rowan tree),
A rowan wreath and a golden curl are the dearest things
  I own,
And to-night, as the sun sinks in the west, I sit and sigh
  alone,
  All in the autumn gloaming.

LOVE'S FAREWELL.

THE ship was ready to leave the shore—
    They stood with their fingers love-entwined.
The tide came in with an angry roar
    (Oh! the wail of the winter wind).
"Though far o'er the ocean I go," said he,
    " Ever with you my love shall dwell."
" And my heart will ever be yours," said she
    (Sad, ah! sad, is love's farewell).

The years have come and the years have gone,
    Bringing tearful eye and clouded brow;
The billows may swell and the tempests moan,
    But the lovers fond are united now.
Tangled and tied rank grasses twine
    Over the maiden's lonely grave ;
And the sailor lies buried beneath the brine
    (Oh! the wash of the wistful wave).

THE MILLER'S DOCHTER.

(After an Old Ballad)

THE miller's dochter 's a winsome quean,
    Bonnie an' fair is she ;
An' to keep the tryst she made yestreen,
She wan'ers doon by the banks sae green—
    And the win' sechs sad thro' the weepin' willow.

She wan'ers on to the auld fute-brig
   (Bonnie an' fair is she);
But the storm is heich, and the burn is big,
An' the auld plank snaps like a rotten twig—
   An' the win' sechs sad thro' the weepin' willow.

The miller's dochter is borne awa'
   (Bonnie and fair is she);
They may search the wud, an' the dell an' a',
But they'll see her nae mair in the miller's ha'—
   An' the win' sechs sad thro' the weepin' willow.

A white swan sails on the burn at nicht,
   Bonnie and fair is she ;
She sings swan-sangs to the mune sae bricht,
Eerie sangs in the pale starlicht—
   An' the win' sechs sad thro' the weepin' willow.

THE SINGERS.

THE cock crawed lood whan the mornin' broke,
   An' struttit aboot whan the worl' awoke ;
He seemed tae be sayin' at every craw—
" A bonnier bird ye never saw !"
   Oh ! hush, thou lood-voiced vaunter, hush !
   For lood i' the woodland waukens the thrush !

The thrush his passionate lyric sung,
An' lood through the woodland the music rung,
An' aye the burden o't seemed tae be—
" Wis there ever a sweeter singer than me ? "
    Oh ! hark, thou passionate singer, hark !
    High up in ether carols the lark !

The lark rose quickly on quiverin' wings,
An' sung as if scornin' a' earthly things ;
His sang seemed tae be, as he mounted higher—
" There is nocht but my music for earth tae admire ! "
    But no ! thou heavenward singer, no !
    There is ane whase sangs hae a sweeter flow !

Oh ! sweet is her sang whan the gloaming grey
Fa's saft owre the earth at the close o' the day ;
An' sweet is the blink o' her bonnie blue e'en—
Earth hasna a fairer than my wee queen !
    Sing on, thou maid o' my heart, sing on !
    My music I find in thy voice alone !

DARKNESS AND LIGHT.

M Y life was full of clouded skies,
        My life was dark as a winter night ;
But I've seen the love-light in your eyes,
        And oh ! but the world is very bright.

My heart was dark—a songless place—
   (Oh ! light and love, I have sought you long)
But now I have seen your winning face,
   And oh ! but the world is full of song.

You came to me like a summer day
   (My life was dark as a winter night),
The gloomy shadows have passed away
   (Oh ! but the world is very bright).

Sweet ! you have brought me untold bliss
   (Oh ! light and love, I have sought you long) ;
A heaven you gave me in that sweet kiss,
   And oh ! but the world is full of song.

THE FISHER'S LASSIE.

I.

TALL an' comely, wi' wavin' hair,
   Doon by the waters o' Morantassie,
Never a kennin' o' wrang or care.
   (A life o' joy for the fisher's lassie).

Lovers seekin' her ilka day
   Roon' by the waters o' Morantassie—
" My fisher-lad I will lo'e for aye !"
   (Simmer a' year for the fisher's lassie).

Village gossips mention her name
  Doon by the waters o' Morantassie,
" A waddin' we 'll hae whan the men come hame.'
  (Ribbons an' braws for the fisher's lassie).

" Lads an' lassies frae faur an' near
  Will come by the waters o' Morantassie,
For, wow, but we lo'e the lassie dear !"
  (A ring o' gowd for the fisher's lassie).

II.

A waesome nicht whan the men come hame—
  Wild the waters o' Morantassie,
Billows black wi' a crest o' faem ;
  (A nicht o' dool for the fisher's lassie).

Lood the thunder the breakers mak',
  Heavin' the waters o' Morantassie,
San's an' rocks a' strewn wi' wrack !
  (Its oh ! an' oh ! for the fisher's lassie).

" Oh ! say, is ma fisher lad safe an' weel—
  Safe frae the waters o' Morantassie ?"
Never a word they answer, I tweel ;
  (A broken he'rt for the fisher's lassie).

Cauld in her room the lassie lies
  Near by the waters o' Morantassie,
Nocht is heard but the sea-birds' cries,
  (Linen white for the fisher's lassie)

TWA MEN.

TWA men gaed intae the Kirk tae pray—
  A rich man an' a puir—
The tane wi' his pridefu' heid held heich,
  The tither booed doon tae the fluir.

The rich man liftit his e'en an' cried;
  "O Lord! I gi'e Thee praise
That I am no like ma neibor-men,
  But haly in a' my ways.

"Swearin' an' swindlin', an' tellin' lees—
  A' thae are things that I hate;
An' a tenth pairt o' ma weekly gains
  On Sunday I pit in the plate."

The puir man prayed an' strak his breist,
  An' never liftit his e'e:
"An' oh! an' oh! I'm a sinner, Lord!
  Be mercifu' tae me!"

The rich man's petition the angels heard—
  Oh! but it pained them sair;
But faur i' the lift there wis haly joy
  At the words o' the puir man's prayer.

———————

WE STRAYED TOGETHER.

FROM the sky fell the lark's soft music showers,
  And the bee hummed over the sweet bell-flowers
    Of the purple heather;
Rich was the scent of the after-math,
Borne on the air to the rugged path
    Where we strayed together.

But ah! all light from our hearts had gone,
Tho' from the flusht heavens the bright sun shone
    O'er the purple heather,
And our eyes were dim with misting tears,
For we knew 'twas the last time for many years
    We would stray together.

Four springs have come to this world of ours—
Four summers have smiled on the scented flowers
    Of the purple heather—
Four autumns have passed in their sober light—
Four winters have covered the fields with white,
    Since we strayed together.

But now you are coming across the sea,
When murmurs the first gold-belted bee
    O'er the purple heather;
And again when the May-birds are fluting clear,
And the May-winds breathe in the woodland fere,
    We will stray together.

LOST LOVE.

HOW often in the days gone by
    I clasped thee in my arms,
And gazed with love-enraptured eye
    On thy enchanting charms—
        Lost love,
    On thy enchanting charms.

For thou wert all the world to me,
    Than all the rest more dear;
The blissful moments spent with thee
    Made summer all the year—
        Lost love,
    Made summer all the year.

But now my dream of love is o'er—
    Such was stern Fate's decree—
Those happy days return no more,
    And I am naught to thee—
        Lost love,
    And I am naught to thee!

ALANE.

I STAN' alane i' the auld kirkyaird,
　　An' my he'rt is fu' o' pain,
As I think on the ane I lo'ed sae weel
　　That frae the dark worl' has gane.
I look on the place whaur we used tae roam
　　Wi' footsteps licht an' free;
But her kin'ly smile an' lovin' look
　　Will beam nae mair on me.
　　　　Willow, willow, her grave is green,
　　　　An' my he'rt, my he'rt is breakin'.

Oh! that dear wee han' that wis laid in mine
　　An' gied sic a joyous thrill!
As I stan' alane in the auld kirkyaird
　　In fancy I feel it still;
But thae smilin' e'en o' heavenly blue
　　Never again will I see,
An' the musical tones o' that gentle voice
　　Will whisper nae mair tae me.
　　　　Willow, willow, her grave is green,
　　　　An' my he'rt, my he'rt is breakin'.

Mine wis her love, that priceless gem;
　　Mine wis her he'rt o' trust;
Alack! alack! that lovin' he'rt
　　Is naething enoo but dust.

In the past days o' youth an' love
  Life seemed sae joyous an' bricht;
But ah! wae's me! owre my spirits noo
  Has fa'en the darkness o' nicht.
    Willow, willow, her grave is green,
    An' my he'rt, my he'rt is breakin'.

ARRAN SONNETS.

—

*To Provost Anderson, Wishaw, these Sonnets are affection-
ately inscribed, in memory of many happily-associated
hours spent in the island of Arran.*

— —

SUMMER IN ARRAN.

" Where the deer rustle through the twining brake
And the birds sing concealed."— *Thomson's Seasons.*

ARRAN, sweet isle of glowing, grassy meads,
    Of giant hills and beauteous flowery dells,
Of starry marigolds and heatherbells,
Of streams that ripple on 'mong marshy reeds,
I love thee. 'Mid the summer's varying moods
    'Tis sweet to roam in some flower-spangled glade,
    Or rest awhile within high Goatfell's shade,
And listen to the music of the woods,
Where Nature's choir hold carnival. 'Tis sweet
    To dwell in some lone, rough-built, rustic cot,
    Where all life's cares may be awhile forgot,
    Where from the city's din we may retreat,
Where burdened hearts and wearied brains may rest
In summer-time. Arran, I love thee best !

HOLY ISLE.

"Dull would he be of soul who could pass by
A sight so touching in its majesty."—*Wordsworth.*

O HEATHER - CINCTURED, tumulose rock
 enisled

By murmuring waves, I love on thee to dream;
I see across the bay the sun-flecked stream
That laves our rustic cot in yonder wild;
On every side the fitful glimmering sea
 Advances and retires with motion slow;
 The tremulous cadence of its ebb and flow
Seems like a wail of human misery.
But all things round their summer beauty wear—
 Over our heads the screaming curlew flies,
 The purple heath with white in sweetness vies,
The trailing blossoms scent the balmy air.
Singing, the boatman waits, with dripping oar,
To waft us back to rugged Arran's shore.

LETTER COTTAGE.

"Here had I favourite stations, where I stood
And heard the murmurs of the ocean flood."— *Crabbe.*

IT was a little cottage near the shore
    In which I dwelt, and often there I heard
The screaming of the foamy-winged sea-bird
Above the ever-sounding billows' roar;
And from its little window I could see
    The huge foam-masses on the brown rocks dash—
    Could see the little village of Lamlash
Curving around the bay.   And memory
Oft dwells upon that scene now far away;
    And in day-dreams I often live again
    Those happy days beside the azure main,
Watching the sea-gulls o'er its bosom play:
And oft there steals upon me in my sleep
The ceaseless, hollow murmur of the deep.

KINGSCROSS.

"Then foremost was the generous Bruce."— *Scott.*

THE Austral stars gleamed brightly when I stood
    At Kingscross, on the rugged, rocky shore,
And brave old stories of the buried yore
The billows seemed to tell in mournful mood;

The sweet, white-bosom'd moon its silvery sheen
  Shed with a southern softness o'er the sea,
  The soft wind sighed in murmurs passion-free,
And fancy called up forms upon the scene ;
Upon the shining shore I seemed to see
  A band of warriors, by their monarch led,
  Launch forth their boats, and in the distance fade,
Their country from th' oppressor's yoke to free.
Long time I, dreaming, stood ; the crimson day
Was slowly breaking as I turned away.

LAMLASH BAY.

> "There is society where none intrudes,
>   By the deep sea, and music in its roar."—*Byron.*

TRANQUILLY gleam the waters of the deep,
  With here and there a distant, snowy sail,
  So lightly gliding in the lustre pale
Of Luna's beams, that on the waters sleep.
Behind me Arran's lofty hills arise,
  Where leap the mountain streams in wanton freaks
  Before me towers the heather-mantled peak
Of Holy Isle, that seems to reach the skies.

Oh! I could ever linger, dreaming here,
 For all around is resting, still and calm—
 No sound intrudes upon the night-winds' balm,
And naught but Fancy's music greets the ear,
When silent moonbeams o'er the waters play,
And sheds the evening-star its genial ray.

KILMORY WATER.

"And rushing and flushing, and brushing and gushing,
 And curling and whirling, and purling and twirling."—Southey.

CURVING and winding thro' the verdant vale
 Kilmory wanders in the green trees' shade,
 While sweetest odours thro' the summer glade
Breathe o'er its waters on the southern gale ;
As soft and silently, as in a dream,
 The boughs bend to the ripples, while a gush
 Of sweetest song from linnet, merle, and thrush
Rings all along the silver-bosom'd stream.
Down from the Arran hills it murmurs free,
 With little cascades making gentle din ;
 Wandering by white Clauchog and Torrylin,
Until it joins its waters with the sea;
Mingling its music with the wilder roar
Of great wave-masses flung upon the shore.

PLADDA LIGHTHOUSE.

"The lighthouse lifts its massive masonry,
  A pillar of fire by night, of cloud by day." *Longfellow.*

HOW sweetly solemn was the scene to me,
    When Pladda lighthouse burst upon my view!
Far from its steadfast, lofty tower it threw
A long red gleam of light across the sea;
And giant ships that passed it in the night—
    Some outward bound and some returning home—
    Their white sails gleaming o'er the restless foam,
Seemed ghost-like as they lingered in the light;
Around its top, with wild and eerie screams,
    The snowy sea-birds flew. The billows crashed
    Against its base, and, rising higher, dashed
Their waters almost to the lantern's beams;
But all immovable it stood the shock,
And shed its welcome gleam from Pladda rock.

A STORM IN ARRAN.

            "Viewless, the winds
With loud, mysterious force the billows sweep,
And sullen roar the surges far below."—*Radcliffe.*

HIGH heave the waters of the troubled main,
    And the green waves dash thro' the Bruce's cave;
Among the hills the mighty thunders rave—
Loud shrieks the wind, and wildly falls the rain;

The little mountain streamlets widely swell.
  And, with hoarse murmurs, rush towards the bay;
  The huge black clouds shut out the light of day,
And hang around the peak of great Goatfell.
Amid the storm I stand upon the shore,
  Until apart the clouds begin to steal —
  Until the thunder sounds its final peal—
Until the streamlets cease their angry roar ;
For in this life, when bitter storms depart,
The calm succeeding soothes the troubled heart.

———————— - - -

GOATFELL.

" O'er the mist-shrouded cliffs of the lone mountain straying."
                                                —*Burns.*

HERE, from the peak of this canescent pile,
    A glorious panorama meets our gaze;
  The distant mountain-peaks, cradled in haze,
The streams, the valleys of this happy isle;
Bright in the summer dayshine, we can see
  The lucent bays, the hills in robes of heath,
  And the long-waving, singing surge, beneath
The tortile clouds trajecting tracery.
Yonder a castellated mansion lies,
  Shrined in the bosom of the verdant hills,
  'Mong woods alive with scented calycles.
O happy isle ! with hungry, longing eyes,
  I gaze upon you ! Ere another day
  I'll tread yon smoky city far away.

FAREWELL TO ARRAN.

> " Bright isle ! might but thine echoes keep
> A tone of my farewell,
> One tender accent, low and deep,
> Shrined 'mid thy rocks to dwell!" *Hemans.*

O FAVOURED, flower-flecked Arran! must I leave
  The summer dwelling to my heart so dear,
For yonder city where I may not hear
The sea's mild, murmuring music morn and eve ?
Ah! yes, the time has come when I must say
  To all your sunny, sea-swept scenes, " farewell!"
  Alas ! that grating grief my heart should swell,
When all around is gleeful, glad, and gay!
Our boat leaves slowly the bipartite bay,
  Severed by Holy Isle's broad baluster—
  O beauteous bay! O isle, infoliate, fair!
Though from your smiling charms I go away,
My heart will still retain your beauties wild,—
Thou sweetest spot by Scotia's seas enisled !

SHINE AND SHADE.

IN MAY.

SWEET the verdant plain,
    Sweet the Summer's smile,
Sweet the country lane,
    Sweet the rustic style,
Sweet by thee to dream—
        Fair stream ;
To dream through all the long warm days,
To hear, not listen—see, not gaze.

Flowing through the mead
    In melodious tune,
Where the oxen feed
    On thy banks at noon,
Often here I come
        To roam ;
To rest among the ripening grass
And watch the silver cloudlets pass.

Fragrant is the air.
    As adown the vale
Feathered songsters fair,
    With their music hail
Summer's blossoms gay —
            'Tis May ;
The meadows wear a starry crown
Green leaves have not yet turned to brown.

Bees hum o'er the flowers ;
    Sweetly flow the brooks,
Singing past fair bowers—
    Curving round sweet nooks.
'Neath the leafy screen
            So green ;
Around me gentle breezes sigh,
As near the streamlet's banks I lie.

Sweet the Autumn bright.
    Sweet the laughing Spring,
Sweet the Winter white—
    Hoary, old Frost-king ;
Sweeter far a day
            In May,
When we can commune, face to face,
With Nature in her brightest dress.

AUTUMN NIGHT.

IN THE COUNTRY.

H OW bright
　　To-night
The stars above us glow,
　　The moonlight beams
　　Upon the streams
That down the hillsides flow :
　On every tree the leaves are shaking.
　Cloud-waves on dusky shores are breaking :
Within the woods no sound is heard : softly the acorns
　　fall
Among the red-leaved undergrowth or fern stems brown
　　and tall :
And Silence over all prevails in her primeval home,
Walled in by clouds and roofed by starry night's gem-
　　spangled dome.

IN THE CITY.

　　The strife
　　Of life
Comes not before our eyes,
　　Heart-hushed, asleep
　　In slumber deep
The busy city lies.
　Gaunt seem the bridges o'er the river,
　That ever flows and murmurs ever.

Upon the silent city the moon looks from on high,
And watches o'er its wealth of souls as with an angel's
    eye;
Across the night's dusk brow the clouds roll on in silv'ry
    bars
And poet-souls grow bright to-night even as the gleaming
    stars.

OCTOBER.

THE sky is grey
    This autumn day,
The cold woods wear an aspect sober,
    But yellow sheaves
    And rustling leaves
A beauty give to brown October.
The scarlet haws and red-leaved brambles, shining bright
    together,
The russet pears, the clover balls, the beauteous purple
    heather,
    These make me love the sober, scented, fragrant
    month October.

    The soft white mist,
    By chill airs kissed,
Over the close-reaped field is sweeping;
    Low sighs the stream,
    The white flocks dream,
The faded year is softly sleeping.

The solemn sunset's golden heaps of clouds so slowly
  waning,
The last sweet minstrel's twittering, the autumn winds'
  soft plaining,
    These make me love the mellow, tranquil, patient
    month October.

ON GLASGOW BRIDGE.

NIGHT'S defluous mantle murked the giant town
        And hushed the din of day,
As on the bridge I lingered, looking down
        Watching the moonlight play.
Mixed with the long-reflected lamplight's shiver
Upon the bosom of the brimming river.

And thus I thought : " How like this river-tide
        Is to our human life !
Born in some distant spot, its waters glide
        Far from the scenes of strife,
Nursed by the summer-song of bird and bee,
Laughing and leaping light in lyric glee.

" Then from the mountain to the meadow green
        Its widening waters flow,
Long lines of lofty, link-limbed trees between
        With course more staid and slow,
With here and there a village by its side,
While rustic arches span its lambent tide.

"And now a city in its course it greets,
    With bridges striding o'er ;
With wondrous wealth of souls, and busy streets
    Of hoarse, heart-wearying roar.
Great ships upon its bosom rest (the fears
And cares that come to us by manhood's years).

"And such has been my life ! such was my youth—
    That pleasant, peaceful flow—
That careless glee   that innocence and truth—
    That laughing long-ago ;
And such is now my life ! the city's din—
The city's snares—the city's sickening sin."

And then I asked myself—"Is this man's doom ?
    This toiling day by day,
This dreary grind with hearts o'ercome with gloom
    That passes not away ;
The gloom that soon o'erflows the weary breast,
Just when we languish most for needed rest ?

" Is this man's doom, that if one try to rise
    Above this dark routine,
Immediately the tempest groans and sighs,
    And biting blasts blow keen ;
And tho' he struggle with o'ermastering fears,
The storm-cloud sunders and he disappears ?

" Is this man's doom,   either a toiling slave
    From morn till gloaming fall,
With ne'er a longing for the great life-wave
    Beyond his prison wall ;

Or else a madman, battling with the gale,
To strive, to strain, to strand, to fag, to fail?"

.   .   .   .

I turned to leave the spot, when lo! the high
Meiosis of the spars
Of the moored shipping led my wistful eye
Up to the gleaming stars—
Up to the diamond-decorated dome,
And soon my heart forgot its cloudy gloom.

" O golden gleams," I cried, " that far above
Our sin-stained planet shine,
That seem fore'er to sing to us the love
Of the Supreme Divine,—
Your glory ever 'dures that we may see
How vast, how vivified our souls might be!"

And in the solemn stillness of the night
That hung around the earth
My soul grew calm, and as the starshine bright;
My thoughts had newer birth;
And I stood nearer the Eternal Throne
Than I had done in all the years bygone.

SUMMER MORN.

NOW from the gleaming blueness overhead
    Have vanished all the night's illumined stars,
  The blushing dawn shines through its golden bars,
The gloom and mystery of night have fled.
Softly and slow the smiling morning breaks,
    The gold-fringed chambers of the east gleam bright,
   And, soaring high to meet the welcome light,
The lark a thankful, joyous song awakes.
Oh! when I turn toward the eastern sky
   And view the beauty of the virgin morn,
   Within my breast what truest joy is born!
To me earth beams with glories from on high,
And echo round me all the summer day
The spirit-hymnings of the Far-away.

SUMMER EVE.

O SUMMER eve! all things are now at rest,
    And thro' the sky's fast-fading purple beams
  The first sweet star: and with his fading gleams
The sun makes glorious all the glowing west.
Entranced I stand, nor heed the passing hours,
   But gaze enraptured on the changing skies,
   While in my breast thoughts of old times arise,
And slow I pass through dreamland's fairy bowers.

O summer eve ! O beauteous crimson sky !
  O setting sun ! O solitary star !
  Your tranquil beauty seems to shed afar
Breathings of holy peace ; yet sad am I—
For ye recall the time I think of most,
When she was tender whom I loved and lost.

ODE FOR THE BURNS ANNIVERSARY.

      "O Burns, to every feeling breast,
        To every gentle mind sincere,
      By love and tender pity blest,
          Thy song is dear."—*Hemans.*

      "Him who lived in glory and in joy,
  Following the plough beneath the mountain's side."
              Wordsworth.

O HUMBLE harp ! over whose fitful strings
    My youthful fingers oft have idly roved,
Help me to sing a name I long have loved—
A name to which my heart in worship clings,
  Whose natal morning now returns—
             BURNS !

He came to us when Scotland's bards
  Had lost their manly tone,
When Scotland's nobles sought rewards
  For flattery of a throne ;
And raised them to a purpose high
In songs the world will ne'er let die.

In lyrics rare he sang the praise
   Of his loved native land,
Which brightened 'neath his rustic lays
   As 'neath a wizard's hand;
And set aglow the youthful fancy
By his heart-charming necromancy!

What truth and tenderness combine,
What power and pathos in every line!
What varied subjects claim his dreams—
The banks and braes, the flowing streams,
The little mouse, the piping thrush,
The daisy 'neath the ploughshare's crush,
The love of " brither bard and frien',"
The love of Mary and bonnie Jean,
The scene in cottage home at night
That sets the lamp of love alight!
His heart was love—his strains reveal
He had no hate even for " The De'il!"

His soulful songs decay forbid,
   His fame will ever stand
Like an eternal pyramid
   Among life's shifting sand!
His mingled pathos, wit, and fire,
All coming ages shall admire!

Not in the little land alone
   That gave the poet birth,
His songs are sung, his name is known
   O'er all the sea-girt earth—

Across the broad Atlantic's wave
In lands Pacific's waters lave.

And from these distant climes
Men who have loved his rhymes
Have to that little green churchyard with reverend foot-
steps come,
And, with low-bending head.
In loving sorrow shed
A tributary tear above poor Burns's early tomb.

Since first he saw the light
Long years have ta'en their flight,
And wrong has striven with right,
And battles have been fought and lost and won ;
And earth has less of night,
And more of sun ;
But the bright laurel green
Around his brow
Is brighter now
Than it in all the years gone bye has been !

Come, then, all loyal-hearted Scots !
" From Maidenkirk to John o' Groats,"
On this our poet's natal day, and worship at the shrine,
Sing loud his never-dying lays,
And weave of everlasting bays
A newer wreath around his noble temples to entwine !

And sing his name,
And his deathless fame.
When the " Januar' win's " are sighing.
The bard is dead—
His soul has fled—
But his song is never-dying !

While breezes soft the sweet bluebell shall woo—
  While on our moors upstarts the sturdy thistle—
  While at the gates of heaven the laverocks whistle—
While woman trusts to man, and man is true—
While o'er the " banks an' braes o' bonnie Doon "
  The rich-songed mavis darts—
While heather scents the smiling summer noon --
  Will BURNS live in our hearts !

And ever as his natal morn returns
Our hearts will tribute pay to glorious BURNS.

O humble harp, over whose fitful strings
  My youthful fingers oft have idly roved,
  When singing of the bard I long have loved
Pleasure unbounded to my heart it brings !

BY THE BAY.

I MUSE alone upon the summer strand ;
  Above me white clouds sail the silent air :
The slow green wave sea-saturates the sand,
  And murmurs like a breath of patient prayer.

The rocks above the bay in long-linked line
    Frown o'er the silver spray along its marge :
The sun's last gleams engild the circling brine,
    And softly sleeps the solitary barge.

How calm and peaceful is this gloaming hour !
    All nature seems soul-rapt in reverie ;
And yet this calm but hides the slumbering power
    That lurks beneath thy singing surge, O sea !

Ah ! silent sea, within thy doomful deep
    A million living things thou nurturest —
Unnumbered lives that swim and swarm and creep
    For ever in a maelstrom of unrest.

Thy undulations nurse the many roots
    Of our wide planet's distant-reaching tree ;
The life that through its spreading branches shoots
    Receives its impulse and its strength from thee.

And thou hast built the rough and ragged rocks,
    And hung them oft with wreck and rack and spar,
And through the centuries thy powerful shocks
    Have rent the island and the main afar.

Oft have I seen thee rising high and high,
    While lightning-flashes leapt from cloud to cloud,
Shrieking and howling while the gloomy sky
    Hung o'er thy foaming waters like a shroud.

And yet so still to-night the bay along,
  Gleaming and glowing in the sunlit space,
I scarce can think of thee—the fierce, the strong—
  That crumblest islands in thy wild embrace.

Alas, man's life is changing storm and calm—
  Peaceful awhile, then frantic storms arise ;
A maniac blaming of the great I AM,—
  Doubt, hate, rage, shame, set with a spume of lies.

In this flusht gloaming hour, so free from strife,
  Thou hast forgot thy storms and wrecks, O sea !
Ah, God, if one pure hour could cleanse man's life,
  How bright and gladsome this dark world would be !

MY HEART.

I ASKED of my heart one summer day,
  When the city streets were crowded and gay,
"O heart of mine ! is this thy home—
In the noisy city with smoky dome,
Its streets that stretch for miles away,
Its masses of homes so stately and gray,
And its river rolling so sullen and slow ?"
      And my heart said : " No !"

" Tell me, my heart, is it where the breeze
Sighs gently through the summer trees,
Where life and beauty are everywhere,
And music is borne on the balmy air—

The song of the birds, the lay of the rills,
The bleat of the lambs on the verdant hills—
Is thy home where the little wild-flowers grow?"
      But my heart said : " No !"

" Is thy home in that land of snowy night,
Where the Northern lights flash and glimmer bright,
Where ocean lies a frozen waste,
And trees by the ice-bands are interlaced,
Where over the land and ocean pale
Rages ofttimes the icy gale—
Is thy home in that clime of frost and snow?"
      But my heart said : " No !"

" Is it, O heart ! 'mong the palmy groves,
Where the terrible lion in freedom roves,
Where tropical plants in their beauty smile,
Where rolls the tide of the swelling Nile ;
Where gentle and aromatic gales
Breathe thro' the fragrant woods and vales,—
Is thy home where such spicy breezes blow?"
      But my heart said : " No !"

" Ah ! heart, my heart, have I guessed the truth?
The maiden I love hath grace and youth—
To me no other seems half so fair,
To me she is sweet beyond compare ;
O heart of mine ! hast thou found thy rest
In the heart that beats in that virtuous breast?—
Oh ! say, is thy home 'neath that bosom of snow?"
      Still my heart said : " No !"

"Then, O my heart! it must surely be
In that land from sorrow and suff'ring free,
Where earthly victors receive their palm,
And join the saints' victorious psalm ;
Is it there, O heart ! thou hast found thy home,
In the land where changes never come—
The realm of eternal happiness?"
   And my heart said : " Yes !" .

THE BEAUTIES OF SPRING.

YE slumb'ring fancies of my soul ! awake,
 And view the new-born beauties of the Spring ;
 List, while the feathered songsters sweetly sing,
Their love-songs making glad each wood and brake.
How beauteous is the Spring-time !   All around
 The trees and fields shine in their emerald hue,
 Above us gleams the sky's resplendent blue,
And in each lane the sweet wild-flowers abound.
The season fills my breast with holy calm ;
 For dark has been the winter, and my heart
 Has shared its gloom.   But now these shades depart,
And all my being joins in Nature's psalm.
Arise ! arise ! my grateful soul, and sing
The praise of Him who sendeth us the Spring.

TO A CAGED LARK.

I GAZE upon thee, and my heart is stirr'd
　　To see thee caged.　With strangely flutt'ring wing
　Thou triest hard to flee thy cage, and sing
The song of freedom.　Ah ! poor little bird !
When on thy wire-bound prison-cage I look
　　There rises to my lips a heart-felt sigh ;
　　Thou should'st be soaring towards the bright blue sky,
Or fluttering o'er some sweetly flowing brook,
Or singing to thy mate thy sweetest song
　　(For ev'n thy bosom feels love's sacred fire) ;
　　But there in doleful prison-house of wire
Thou hast been long confined ; O monstrous wrong !
Had I the power, poor bird, thou should'st be free,
And he, thy jailer, in thy place should'st be.

UNDER THE OLD OAK TREE.

OH WELL I remember that warm June day,
　　When the sun shone bright on the daisied lea ;
We sat together, my love and I,
　　　　Under the old oak tree.

The light breezes played with her dark brown hair—
　　Was there ever a maiden so fair as she ?
Was there ever a sweeter than she I clasped
　　　　Under the old oak tree ?

A thrush sang loud in the boughs o'erhead,
   I echoed its song in my heart with glee;
For was not the maiden I loved by my side,
      Under the old oak tree?

Oh! well I remember the question I asked,
   With pleading voice and with bended knee,
While her face flushed rosy-red—love's own tint—
      Under the old oak tree.

'Twas only a simple word she said—
   But, oh! how sweet was that word to me;
And sweet was the kiss I stole that day,
      Under the old oak tree.

SUMMER JOYS.

OH, SWEET is the air this summer day,
   The birds are singing on every spray;
Over the lily-bells hum the bees,
Soft sighs the wind thro' the leaf-laden trees:
Those strains, so soft and musical, move
My weary and desolate heart to love!

Oh! how I love to ramble for hours
To gaze on the green leaves, the buds, and the flowers;
To watch, enraptured, the dazzling gleam
Of the sun's bright rays on the rippling stream:

Those sights, so sweet and beautiful, move
My weary and desolate heart to love !

Oh ! sad was the time when the wintry air
Left the trees unleaved and the pastures bare ;
When the biting wind, and the frost, and the rain
Had banished the flowers from the rustic lane ;
O summer, so sweet, your beauties move
My weary and desolate heart to love !

"WHERE MANY-TINTED WILD FLOWERS BLOOM."

WHERE many-tinted wild flowers bloom I lie ;
    Around the spot sweet waving grasses grow,
And 'mong the corn the scarlet poppies glow ;
The soft west winds in gentle murmurs sigh
    Among the yellow corn and ripening wheat,
    And nature's joy seems full and most complete ;
But not for me, for ah ! thou art not by.
    How pleasant was the time when we twain strayed
    In summer through the wood, the lane, and glade,
When not a cloud of sorrow dimm'd our sky.
    O sweet, sweet days, I dream ye o'er again ;
    Such dreaming brings me pleasure, brings me pain:
Pleasure, for once again thou seemest nigh,
But soon the dream flies, then I sadly sigh.

JOHN HOWARD PAYNE.

[John Howard Payne, the author of the well-known "Home, Sweet Home," was born in New York, in the year 1792, and died in Africa, towards the close of 1852. He never knew the comforts of a home, but led a wandering life—often suffering the greatest privations. The following is taken from one of his letters:— "How often I have been in Paris, Berlin, London, and other cities, and heard persons singing and hand-organs playing 'Home, Sweet Home,' without a shilling to pay the next meal, or a place to lay my head! The world has generally sung it until every heart is familiar with its melody, yet I have been a wanderer from my boyhood." Since the following was written, steps have been taken for the removal of the poet's remains to New York, where handsome subscriptions have been raised towards erecting a monument to his memory.]

HOW oft the sweet soft strains of "Home, Sweet Home,"
Have been breathed forth by voices full of glee,
And yet the joys of home were not for thee—
A wand'rer o'er the wide earth thou did'st roam.
Poor Payne! that such thy destiny should be
Never to know that source of joy and rest
Where busy man retires with peaceful breast
From the day's troubles and its trials free;
No marble marks the spot where thou dost lie,
And yet thou hast a lasting monument
Within our hearts. Thy strains were surely sent
From Heav'n to cheer the wounded hearts that sigh;
And surely when thy wand'rings here were o'er,
Thy "Home, Sweet Home," was on Heav'n's shining shore.

SUMMER'S CROWN HAS FALLEN.

SUMMER'S crown has fallen—
  Summer's crown of roses;
On the quiet earth
  Dreamy light reposes.

At the break of day
  Heavy dews are lying;
Thro' the fading trees
  Mournful winds are sighing.

Sweet the robins' notes
  From the plantain issue;
Shining 'mong the trees
  Floats the spider's tissue.

On the quiet earth
  Dreamy light reposes;
Summer's crown has fallen —
  Summer's crown of roses.

QUESTIONINGS.

LINGER, ye gleaming stars of night, why should ye
fade away?

        "To bring the day!"

Linger, ye snowflakes, why thus come to fade away
again?

        "That Spring may reign!"

Linger, ye blossoms, why should ye be part of Autumn's
loot?

        "To bring the fruit!"

Linger, O years! why must we all pass thro' the Vale
of Gloom?

        "That life may come!"

WHAT USED TO BE.

WHEN the sun thro' the branches was weaving
A web of bright colour and gold,
When the spring-blown old orchard was heaving,
Oft down the bright garden we strolled,
And I plucked you the spring flowers so fair,
        Ma chère,
To place in the folds of your hair.

Then you went to your home in the city,
    And the garden's spring beauty was o'er;
You mixed with the clever and witty,
    And came to my side no more.
      Arcadia for you had no spell,
                Ma belle,
    Nor the spring flowers I loved so well.

Still I hum to myself in the gloaming
    The ballads you used to sing,
When together, so leisurely roaming,
    We went in that vanished spring.
      'Tis only a vision to see,
                Ma mie,
    Just a dream of what used to be.

TWO PRAYERS.

A PRAYER went up to heaven in the night
  From a heart that had failed in the world's hard
    fight :
          "Oh! for the time
          When hands shall rest
          And eyes be ne'er
          By grief oppressed ;
          When sighing lips
          Shall be at peace,
          When all life's cares
          And gloom shall cease!"

But the heart had triumphed, for this was the prayer
That was sent aloft in the morning air:
    " Father, forgive !
    My hands shall still
    Labour and strive
    To do Thy will:
    No more my eyes
    Will dim with tears,
    No more my lips
    Breathe griefs and fears!"

WHERE THE STREAM MEETS THE LAKE.

    THE birds are singing,
      Their music flinging
Over the breast of the slumberous lake;
    The drooping willows
    Hang o'er the billows;
Dreamiest music the wild bees make ;
And her blue eyes look tenderly into mine,
While a sweet wild rose in her hair I twine.

    Over the pebbles,
    In silvery trebles,
The streamlet dances in wild unrest ;
    The sun declining
    Is richly shining,
Gilding with glory the gleaming west ;
And she whispers, " I'll wear the flower for your sake,"
Oh! sweet, sweet spot, where the stream meets the lake !

"OH! FOR THOSE HAPPY DAYS."

OH FOR those happy days of which we read,
   Those vanished days of which the poets dream—
When gods were lying by each silv'ry stream,
Or ling'ring, laughing, in each dewy mead.
  Those unsophisticated, olden days
   Have long since vanished, and our present ways
Accord not with that sweet simplicity.
Why do I sigh for that which cannot be?
There is a reason.   'Tis that she I love,
   With quiet bosom, calm and untouched heart,
   Might, like the maids of old, by Cupid's dart
Be pierced while wand'ring in the summer grove;
For though I love her, no responsive chord
Vibrates within her heart, so chill and hard.

HOPE, FANCY, JOY, AND LOVE.

IN youth's sweet morn, amid my cherished dreams,
   I seemed to see around my rugged path
Sweet angel forms, whose influence sent gleams
   Of light across the dark hours childhood hath.
Among these visions, chiefest of them all,
   Were smiling Hope, sweet Joy, and blessed Love,
   And wild-winged Fancy, which would ofttimes rove,
Though each was ever ready at my call.

But as I older grow, I sometimes find
    That tho' Hope o'er my heart still holds its sway,
    Still Joy will oft desert me on my way,
And Fancy lingers often far behind ;
    And Love, sweet Love, altho' I deemed it best,
    I gave in keeping to another breast.

DREAMING EYES.

YOU sit with a far-off look in your eyes,
    And your thoughts are far away ;
In a world of dreams that I cannot know
    Your fancies for ever stray.
'Tis the longing of love in your eyes I see,
And, sweet, I know you are lost to me.

I fancied awhile that those violet eyes
    Were beaming alone for me ;
And now my hopes to the earth are dashed
    (And it's oh ! for the years to be) :
But the wearyful world will never know
That my life for ever has lost its glow.

THE WHISPERING WIND.

THE wind is whispering
    Soft in the grove,
Tenderly whispering
    Of one I love :

Tell me, O wind! does she dream of me
Is she in sadness, or is she in glee?

The wind is sighing—
Ah! heart, ah! heart;
Is the wind telling
That we must part?
Why art thou sighing, O wandering wind?
Has she forgot me, who once was kind?

The wind is moaning
As if to say:
"Your hearts are sundered,
And drifting away!"
O cruel wind, should this thing be,
What, oh what, would be life to me?

"I KNOW A FACE."

I KNOW a face,
Crowned with clustering hair,
Love's youthful grace
Beams there;
A face on which the lily glows
And mingles with the crimson rose.

I know bright eyes,
　So fervent, clear, and true ;
　　Like summer skies,
　　　As blue ;
A heavenly empire is each eye,
Each look an angel from on high.

I know a voice
　That soft responds to mine ;
　　Maid of my choice,
　　　'Tis thine !
That voice so tender, sweet, and true,
That softly whispered, "I love you!"

WHAT I GAVE HER.

I GAVE my love a little flower—
　　A flower of colour gay,
It bloomed on her breast until it died,
　　And then it was cast away ;
　　　O flower so bright,
　　　Now is the night,
And you have bloomed your day !

I gave my love a loving heart—
　　A heart that was full of trust,
It lay in her little hand a while,
　　But now it is in the dust ;

A woman's mind
Is as the wind ;
Die, heart, for die you must !

"O HAPPY DREAMLAND."

O HAPPY dreamland, sweet thy magic spell,
    When in bright visions (all too sweet to last)
We see fair pictures of the joyous past
That with a dazzling glow before us swell.
Old memories a gleeful glamour throw
    Around our spirits, and before our eyes,
    Smiling, the well-remembered shadows rise—
Shadows of those we cherished long ago.
To the sad earthworn soul they come like gleams
    Of heavenly rest, and with sweet peace they fill
    Our aching hearts.   What blissful feelings thrill
Our breasts while wand'ring in the realms of dreams !
But, ah ! those joys that haunt us in our sleep
Soon vanish, and we ofttimes wake to weep.

A VIOLET.

HERE, on the grassy bank of this green lane,
    In tender beauty blooming at my feet,
I've found the year's first violet—so sweet
And bright—refreshened by the welcome rain

Fain would I pluck thee, floweret, for my fair
  To shed thy modest beauty on the breast
  Of her I fondly love, or softly rest
Among the wavelets of her gleaming hair.
The music of the woodlands thou would'st miss,
  And ev'ning winds that softly o'er thee fleet ;
  But ah ! my loved one's voice is passing sweet—
Sweeter than Zephyr is her loving kiss.
Soon with the spring thy beauteous tints will fly—
Would'st thou not rather in her presence die ?

A SIGH.

" The remembrance of youth is a sigh."—Aci.

I SIT by the fire at the midnight's dark hour,
  And I think of the days long gone by ;
A feeling of sadness comes over my soul
  " The remembrance of youth is a sigh !"

I think of those school-days, so happy and free,
  When sorrow ne'er dimmed the young eye :
But, ah ! those sweet days never more can return —
  " The remembrance of youth is a sigh !"

In youth, life's sweet summer of pleasure and joy,
  No one was more happy than I ;
But changes have come, these bright days long have fled
  " The remembrance of youth is a sigh !"

And now, 'mid the cares and the troubles of life,
　Temptations and snares ever nigh,
I sigh for the vanished spring-time of my youth,—
　"The remembrance of youth is a sigh!"

And even tho' sunshine beams forth now and then,
　And pleasures around us may lie,
The heart backwards turns to the sweet days of yore,—
　"The remembrance of youth is a sigh!"

———

SUMMER IN THE CITY.

'TIS summer in the city, and the throng
　　Enjoying the bright sunshine pass along.
Through court and alley, lane and busy street,
We hear the trampling of a thousand feet.
The children find out where the sunbeams glance,
And, gleeful, in the golden arrows dance;
But in the streets each lofty spire and wall
A dark and gloomy shadow throws o'er all.
We miss the music of the rippling rill —
Our only flowers are on the window sill;
No fields, no hedgerows meet the anxious eye—
The dark, dense smoke shuts out the azure sky.
The sight of worldly men pursuing gain
Fills us with longing for the fields again.

SUMMER IN THE COUNTRY.

HOW sweet in summer is a rustic scene,
  The hedgerows, trees, and fields of lucid green,
The flowers in modest beauty at our feet,
The sylvan songsters warbling music sweet.
O'er all the tree-tops gleams the liquid light,
O'er all the hill-sides shine the daisies white,
O'er all the meadows breathes the fresh, pure air,
And gently winds the brooklet cool and fair.
The summer sun is glancing warm and bright,
We listen to earth's music with delight.
Oh happy must they be and sweet their lot
To pass their lives in some sweet rustic cot :
How sweet such shaded, scented lanes to rove !
How sweet such scenes for whisperings of love !

TO MY SISTER—MRS. BISSET.

YOU say that my songs are plaintive and sad,
  And full of a wild unrest ;
Yet they breathe but those feelings that, phantom-like,
  Flit oftentimes through my breast.

When sunshine has fled and the earth is all gloom,
  We hear not the song of the lark ;
But the heart that is thirsting and longing for light
  Must sigh forth its song in the dark.

5

And many a soul, 'mid the battle of life,
   Has been riven by sorrow's keen dart;
So these plaintive breathings of mine may find
   An echo in some kindred heart.

IN THE WOODS.

I LOVE to wander in the silent wood,
   No sound save soft winds sighing through the trees,
The song of birds, or humming of the bees;
Nought else to break the calm of solitude—
Where oaks, and elms, and dark firs stand erect,
Where the sweet daisy and the primrose fair,
And trailing brambles scent the summer air,
And humblest flowers God's love and care reflect.
When opening buds bloom fair at early morn,
And little spring-flowers sparkle on the lea,
I love to stand beneath some huge oak tree,
With sweetest odours on the soft wind borne;
'Tis then solemnity may clasp the soul
And point it to a nobler, higher goal.

WEARY.

THE hills are deckt wi' a starry croon,
   The air is sweet wi' the odour o' June,
Balmiest beauty lies a' aroon';
   But, oh! an' my he'rt is weary.

The keen, cauld breath o' winter has gane,
An' pleasant summer has come again ;
Flooers bloom in the meadow, the wud, an' lane :
But, oh ! an' my he'rt is weary.

Sair is the fecht in the battle o' life,
Doubtings, defeats, an' dangers rife ;
Ill ha'e I fared in the earthly strife,
An' oh ! but my he'rt is weary.

Oh ! when life's gloamin' shall roon' me creep,
An' I hear the dash o' the water sae deep,
I 'll welcome wi' joy the lang, last sleep,
For oh ! but my he'rt is weary.

BY-AND-BYE.

AH me,
  Rough is the way ;
  And I can never see
The dawning of that glorious day
When blissful rest shall come to those who sigh—
The everlasting rest of that sweet by-and-bye.

The wind
In sadness wails,
I can no pleasure find
In song of birds—their sweetness fails,

My spirit yearns for that bright land on high ;
No sin, no sorrow there, in that sweet by-and-bye.

O dove,
For thy swift wing
To reach that land of love
Where sin-freed spirits sweetly sing !
Oh, for that rest, that home beyond the sky,
The peace, the love, the joy of that sweet by-and-bye !

THE WORLD.

" THE world is sweet," said the careless child,
As he roamed through the mountain glens blythe
and wild.

" The world is bright," said the hopeful youth,
And life seemed to him to be fraught with truth.

" The world is hard," said the toiling wight,
As he turned him again to its labour and fight.

" The world is cold," said the hoary sage,
As he thought of the troubles that come with age.

" The world is naught," saith a comforting voice,
" Then heavenward turn, and forever rejoice."

I HEARD THEE SING.

I HEARD thee sing what time my soul was faint,
　　When life's annoyances had clasped my heart ;
　　When sick of earth's false joys and slavish art,
When I had none to hear my mournful plaint.
I heard thee sing, and oh ! the soothing strain,
　　So ravishingly soft, so plaintive, sweet,
　　With melting calm my spirit seemed to greet,
And cool with heavenly peace my fevered brain.
Such power as thine is surely sent from Heaven
　　To brighten dark spots in the vale of life,
　　To free the weary heart from worldly strife,
To cheer the soul by envy's darts deep riven ;
Be this thy aim, and when life's last gleam flies,
I'd wish thee near to sing me to the skies.

BLOW SOFT, YE GENTLE ZEPHYRS.

BLOW soft, ye gentle zephyrs of the night !
　　Sigh gently through the summer-scented grove,
　　And bear a message to the one I love.
Tell her that though far distant from my sight,
　　My loving heart is her's and her's alone ;
　　Murmur my message in a tender tone,

And with thy gentliest kisses touch her face.
   Never, O gentle zephyrs, have ye met
   Such coral lips, such hair of gleaming jet;
Ne'er hast thou kissed a form so full of grace,
And not on earth her equal could ye find.
   Hover around her, fill her heart with glee,
   And when she dreams, oh! bid her dream of me.
See that thou bear'st my message right, O wind!

WHERE THE FERNS GROW.

IN quiet nooks,
   Where flow the summer brooks,
Or in the forests at the great trees' feet—
   A sweet retreat—
   Grow the ferns.

In cool dark caves,
   Whose walls the streamlet laves,
Even where the giant rocks are towering steepest
   And glooming deepest,
   Grow the ferns.

Where no one sees
   Them bending to the breeze,
Sheltered by some old ruin grim and hoary,
   In summer glory
   Grow the ferns.

No sweet perfume,
No soul enchanting bloom,
Hath Nature granted to this beauteous race,
Yet sweetest grace
Have the ferns.

SUMMER IS GOING.

SUMMER'S flowers and summer's joys
   Soon will leave us,
Winter's cold and winter's gloom
   Come to grieve us ;
  The leaves, the grass,
   The flowers will die,
   I can but sigh—
  " Alas ! alas !"

Even now the chilly winds
   Soft are sighing,
And the birds to other lands
   Swift are flying.
  So pleasures pass
   And friendships die ;
   I can but sigh—
  " Alas ! alas !"

ACROSTIC TO BABY MINNIE.

M AY no dark cloud obscure thy life's sweet day,
    Infinite love surround thee on thy way;
No anxious cares or vexing griefs annoy,
Nor aught occur to mar thy life's pure joy;
In thee may love and gentleness combine—
Eternal peace and happiness be thine!

BABY MINNIE'S BIRTHDAY.

H APPY may thy birthday be!
    May this day, my little maiden,
    With the summer breeze balm-laden,
Be an omen bright to thee.

Cares and troubles pass thee by—
    Without care thy heart is beating,
    Heeding not how time is fleeting—
Not a cloud obscures thy sky.

Fraught with love and joy and glee,
    Undisturbed by woe or sadness,
    But replete with mirth and gladness,
May each future birthday be.

LOVE.

'TIS sweet
        At eve to meet
A maiden fair, to roam the fields among,
        To dream
        By some fair stream,
And whisper tales of love with artless tongue.

        At night,
        By Cynthia's light,
When everything in nature is at rest,
        'Tis sweet,
        'Tis joy complete,
To strain a little darling to your breast.

        'Tis bliss
        To steal a kiss,
To feel true love within your bosom burn ;
        Ah ! yes,
        'Tis happiness
To love and be beloved in return.

        'Tis joy,
        Without alloy,
To feel a loving woman's fond caress ;
        O love !
        Sent from above,
Thou mak'st an Eden of life's wilderness.

OLD YEAR, FAREWELL.

OLD year, farewell!
      You cannot stay—must needs away—
Time waves his hand, and you obey.

      Old year, farewell!
You brought us sorrow, brought us woe,
And yet we sigh to see thee go.

      Old year, farewell!
The seeds we 've sown while thou wast here
May blossom in some future year,
Bringing comfort, bringing cheer,
Or causing many a burning tear.

      Old year, farewell!
You brought us sorrow, brought us woe,
The good you brought we hardly know;
We see the worst—'tis always so—
And yet we're sad to see thee go.

MIGHT HAVE BEEN.

WHEN I sit by the fire in the evening's grey,
      Before me flit many a changing scene,
Pict res that burn themselves into my brain—
      Of a wasted youth—of a " might have been."

Time was when my thoughts to the future would turn,
    When patient-eyed Hope in my breast was queen ;
But malice remembered, and envious tongues
    Full oft showed me all that I might have been.

Oh ! why will the world remember ill,
    And ne'er let the good that men do be seen,
But treasure up evil, and gloatingly talk
    Of people's misdeeds, and what might have been !

Like the Priest and the Levite, my friends pass by,
    As if from an outcast, a thing unclean ;
At the sound of my name they look pityingly,
    And talk of the things that I might have been.

But their taunts will be vain when I 'm laid in the grave,
    And the grass o'er my breast shines in lucid green ;
Unheeded they 'll be, though they speak with disdain,
    Or sneeringly whisper, " He might have been."

No one will know of my anguish at times,
    Of the pangs of remorse, of the tears unseen ;
No one will know of my hopes and fears,
    Nor my own sad dreams of what might have been.

Ah, sad it will be to die lonely, unmourned,
    And sad to have never a tear, I ween ;
Yet friends might have thought of the lost one in love,
    If things had been as they might have been.

"WHEN SOL WAS SETTING."

WHEN Sol was setting in the west
    And crimsoning the skies,
I hied me thro' the summer wood
    As but a lover hies.
"O young green leaves, so soft, so sweet,"
    I sang with youthful glee;
" Ye 're very fair, but she I love
    Is fairer far to me."

The little birds on every bough
    Their feathered mates soft wooed,
The merle poured forth his passionate strain,
    The gentler cushat cooed.
"O joyous birds," I sang again,
    " Your songs are gay and free;
But the love-breathings of my fair
    Are sweeter strains to me."

" O young green leaves, so soft, so sweet,
    O beauteous leaves, so fair,
O joyous birds, whose songs of love
    Enrich the summer air,
When winter comes with chilling breath
    Your charms away have passed;
But she I love will still be near,
    And love while life shall last!"

"NOW I LAY ME DOWN TO SLEEP!"

I.

BY a patient mother's knee,
   White-robed, kneeling lowly,
Innocent and trouble-free,
   Praying soft and slowly:
"Now I lay me down to sleep,
I pray the Lord my soul to keep!"

II.

Mingling with earth's toil and fight—
   Of life's troubles weary;
Praying ever thus at night,
   Though the day be dreary:
"Now I lay me down to sleep,
I pray the Lord my soul to keep!"

III.

Trusting still to One above,
   Even when weak and dying,
Leaning on His wondrous love,
   With her last breath sighing:
"Now I lay me down to sleep,
I pray the Lord my soul to keep!"

WAKING.

THE bright sun is waking, my love, my love,
    And crimson the east is glowing;
The cold stars are fading, my love, my love,
    Soft morning breezes are blowing.
        Far in the east
        The day is breaking;
        Yes! the bright sun
        Is waking!

The minstrels are waking, my love, my love,
    Blackbird and throstle and linnet;
And the gay chorus, my love, my love,
    Grows louder every minute.
        Songs full of glee
        The birds are making;
        Yes! the sweet birds
        Are waking!

The roses are waking, my love, my love,
    Roses with dew-gems gleaming;
Roses sweet-tinted, my love, my love,
    In the rosy dawn-light dreaming.
        On ev'ry spray
        The buds are breaking;
        Yes! the sweet roses
        Are waking!

Oh ! art thou waking, my love, my love,
  Or art thou still softly sleeping ?
Yes ! thou art waking, my love, my love,
  From thy casement I see thee peeping !
      Sweet joy my heart
      Is now partaking,
      For thou, my love,
      Art waking !

"MINNIE GAVE TO ME."

WHEN the west's rich amber
  Deepened into grey,
When was hushed the thrush's
  Wild impromptu lay—
Standing there together,
  'Neath the old beech tree,
Oh ! the loving glances
  Minnie gave to me !

Darker fell the gloaming
  Over glade and hill—
Save the whispering breezes,
  Everything was still ;
Than the rest of nature
  Happier were we—
Oh ! the words of sweetness
  Minnie gave to me !

Night-mists swiftly gathered,
  And above us soon,
Through a sea of glory,
  Sailed the silver moon ;
With our arms entwining,
  'Neath the old beech tree,
Oh ! the honey kisses
  Minnie gave to me !

TO MY FRIEND ANGUS ROSS.

AS life's rough thorny road we pass alang, Angus Ross,
    Wi' griefs an' cares we 're keepit unco thrang,
  Angus Ross,
        Yet aye we fin' relief,
        Frae ilka woe an' grief,
In the liltin' o' a canty, hamely sang, Angus Ross.

An' ye ha'e gi'en us mony sic-like lays, Angus Ross,
An' weel deserve oor he'rtfelt thanks an' praise, Angus
  Ross,
        Wi' sangs o' wud an' grove—
        O' lasses an' o' love—
Richt weel ye 've won the poet's lasting bays, Angus Ross.

Though young, I 've shared the sorrows o' life's road,
  Angus Ross,
An' aften felt misfortune's cruel goad, Angus Ross ;
        But when at day's decline
        I read thae sangs o' thine,
My he'rt is lichtened o' its weary load, Angus Ross.

Though M—— frae his lofty heicht looks doon, Angus
    Ross,
An' for "wee bards" has naething but a froon, Angus
    Ross,
        The humble lilt imparts
        A joy tae mony hearts
That ne'er were thrilled wi' lays o' grander soon', Angus
    Ross.

Sae let the muses still your worship claim, Angus Ross,
Such pure an' lofty strains be still your aim, Angus Ross,
        An' when in weel-earned peace
        Your earthly labours cease,
Ye 'll haud a place upon the roll o' fame, Angus Ross.

—————

THE RAINBOW'S LESSON.

IN the west, the beams of the setting sun
    Their glorious crimson spread;
In the east, a feathery vapour-cloud
    Rose gradually overhead;
When lo! a bright rainbow the heavens spanned,
As if raised by the touch of enchanter's wand!

The sunset, the cloud, the tinted arch,
    Have brought a lesson to me,
For shadowing troubles have clouded my soul
    And the meaning I could not see;

6

But the lesson I learnt from the east and west
Has brought to my troubled bosom rest.

We may meet with clouds in this life of ours—
   Trials and doubts will come ;
But the love of God, like the sun's bright glow,
   Brightens the tearful gloom.
I had ofttimes prayed from the clouds to be free—
Lord ! if thou wilt, let them stay with me.

THE LASSIE I LOVE.

HOW sweet to my ear is the sang o' the birds,
   When summer enlivens each woodland and grove ;
But the sang I like best at the close o' the day,
   Is some auld Scottish lilt frae the lassie I love.

Oh ! dear to my heart are the ballads an' sangs
   That leal Scottish bards o' the ancient times wove,
But dearer by far, an' aye sweeter they seem,
   When sung owre to me by the lassie I love.

Let rhymesters wha will, sing o' mountain and plain,
   I carena in such paths to let my muse rove ;
I 'll sing o' the joys o' the sweet gloamin' hour
   When I meet in the glen wi' the lassie I love.

Awa' wi' sic rhymes, they're but fusionless stuff,
　They warm na' the bluid, nor the loving heart move :
Na, na, I will sing o' a theme better far—
　The bonnie blue e'en o' the lassie I love.

She's winsome an' bonnie, she's modest and true,
　She's lovin' an' kind, an' as gentle's the dove :
May troubles owrecome me, and fortune forsake,
　If ever I leave the sweet lassie I love.

'Tho' flichty young things at my notions may sneer.
　An' auld folk may shake their wise heads an' reprove,
While there's sight to my e'en, while my haun' hauds the
　　pen.
　I 'll write in the praise o' the lassie I love.

DO YOU REMEMBER?

DO you remember the lovers' green lane,
　　The seat 'neath the old oaken tree ?
Do you remember those bright, happy days,—
　Who were so happy as we ?
Sitting together and whispering low—
Do you remember that long, long ago ?

Do you remember the vows that we made ?
　How lovingly hand clasped hand ?
Do you remember the kisses you gave,
　When at the gate we would stand ?

Loving so truly, with no thought of woe,—
Do you remember that long, long ago?

Do you remember our joy, love, to meet?
  Our sorrow when we had to part?
Do you remember the sweet balmy eve
  I clasped you as mine to my heart?
Pleasures we knew only lovers can know,—
Do you remember that long, long ago?

Do you remember my going away
  Far o'er the rude ocean's foam?
Do you remember our sad, sad farewell
  When leaving my loved childhood's home?
Now that I'm home again, no more to go,
We will repeat, love, that long ago.

A FROZEN STREAM.

I LOVE to gaze upon a frozen stream,
  So silent and so pure, so bright and fair,
When chill and piercing is the wintry air,
When faint and cheerless is the wintry beam.
No voice is heard within the stilly wood,
  The birds have sought a home far o'er the sea:
  No green leaves hang on bush or giant tree,
And all around is deepest solitude.

So picturesque the scene—so calm and light,
  No wonder 'tis the artist's constant theme;
So cold and still, and yet withal so bright,
  How meet to be the source of poet's dream :
And tho' death's image this still stream may be,
Beneath the surface cold it ripples free.

LOVE'S PLEADING.

THE western sky with crimson light is gleaming,
  The feathered songsters warble in the grove :
O'er hill and dale their joyful notes are streaming—
  Stay with me yet awhile, my life, my love !

Sweet through the summer air we hear their voices.
  The joyous thrush, the gentle turtle-dove ;
All nature in the beauteous light rejoices—
  Stay with me yet awhile, my life, my love !

Linger till Cynthia bright, serenely sailing,
  Behind the passing clouds shall quickly move,
As if from earthly gaze her beauty veiling—
  Stay with me yet awhile, my life, my love !

When night's dark garment all the still earth covers,
  And fiery stars are gleaming bright above,
That is the moment sweet to dreaming lovers—
  Stay with me yet awhile, my life, my love !

CHANGES.

THE night
Gives place to light,
Earth leaves her murky pall,
And morning's gold gleams over all.

O'er earth,
In hideous mirth,
The storm-fiends laugh and wail :
But calm succeeds the fiercest gale.

What drear
And dismal cheer
The days of winter bring ;
But these give place to smiling spring.

And life,
With all its strife,
Has still that morn of peace
Whose bliss and joy will never cease.

THE APPROACH OF SPRING.

AFTER winter's cold and tempest,
After winter's sorrowing,
Gladdening all the wistful meadows,
Comes the smiling spring

In a garb of ever-changing
  Emerald and amethyst,
Round her form her tresses flowing,
  By the zephyrs kissed.

Rubies in their glory glowing
  'Mid her folds of gleaming hair,
Opals with their hidden roses
  On her bosom fair.

Earth grows bright at her approaching,
  Spring the cowslips amber-hued,
Daisies dapple all the meadows,
  Bluebells star the wood.

From the shelter comes a pæan
  Of exultant, thankful song;
Linnet, chaffinch, thrush, and blackbird
  Sing the boughs among.

And our spirits, winter-weary,
  Join the song the minstrels sing ;
Join the opening flowers' worship,
  Welcoming the spring !

A NOCTURNE.

THE setting sun's abrading roseate bloom
  Engilds the sky beyond the western height,
Acervous clouds grow dark, and with the gloom
  Submissive day yields to the silent night.

One more admovent day, on flightful wings,
Passes away to be with bygone things !

Heaven's lights are out, and o'er the blue vast weave,
    In far festoons, the stars' fixed fearless fires,
That show embossed upon the front of eve
    The lofty towers and high aculeate spires,
And palely show, in faintest adumbration,
The stately streets in lengthy catenation.

The crescent moon, a curve of burnished gold,
    Amid the fleecy clouds sublimely floats ;
The wind, that sung earth's cradle-hymns of old,
    Sends o'er the city its canorous notes ;
Why should a time like this—so full of rest—
Awaken shadowing thoughts within my breast ?

These worlds, that glimmer with dilucid glow,
    Whose glistering gleams make glad the midnight's
      gloom,
Must they, too, share the life—the strife—the woe—
    Of this earth deodand—and share its doom ?
Must they with our devitiated world
Be downward into dire destruction hurled ?

Oh ! troubling thoughts away ! for though 'tis hard
    To think of sin in any world space-nursed,
'Tis best to trust that these are still unmarred,
    Not like our planet, vile and sin-accursed ;
That they are free from earth's nigrescent night—
Earth's carious joys and deathful aconite !

So when I see the starshine brightly gleam,
  The white advening roof of cloud above,
Sinless and pure these worlds I will addeem—
  Full of our God, His life, and light, and love;
And then my soul shall leave this world of care,
And hold communion with its Maker there !

IN MONKLAN' GLEN.

I SEE it yet ! dear Monklan' Glen.
    The trees sae dark an' green,
The grassy knowes, the flooer-decked banks.
    The bonnie burn between.
I see it yet ! the auld beech tree,
    Its leaf-clad branches spread
Like strong protectin' arms abune
    The yellow primrose bed.

I see her yet ! the bonnie lass,
    Wha wan'ered wi' me there ;
I see the modest. smilin' face
    Aneath the dark-broon hair.
I see her yet ! her image is
    Engraved upon my he'rt ;
I lo'ed her weel, but cruel fate
    Ordained that we should pairt.

Some ane has said (an' on his words
    My mem'ry fondly dwells),
" Oor angels are the anes we lo'e—
    Oor Heaven lies wi' oorsel's."
I sometimes think my angel is
    A lass I used tae ken—
My Heaven aneath an auld beech tree
    In bonnie Monklan' Glen.

CASTLE SONNETS.

STRATHAVEN CASTLE.

A LONELY tower upon a grassy steep,
   Up which we climb among the towering trees,
  Where, shaded half, and half revealed, one sees
The noiseful waters of Pomillon sweep;
And o'er the stream the humble cottage walls
  Of those who, oft in times of fight and fray,
  By gloomy stair and subterraneous way,
Came to the shelter of the castle's halls.
Ah! gallant hearts, when Scotland's peace was marred,
  Ye held your own against invading foes,
  Gaining her freedom—grand, triumphal close!
And now sleep well within the old churchyard;
Swathed in the verdure of long centuries;
Soothed by the river's faint antiphonies.

BOTHWELL CASTLE.

SPRING, summer, autumn, winter, weave their way
   Like dancers in a stately minuet ;
  The sun still shines with daily rise and set ;
The world still rolls alternate night and day ;
But peoples change. Those rude, red, rugged towers
   Have seen such days as we can only dream ;
   Those quiet walls, that willowy-winding stream,
Have heard the clangour of contending powers ;
And now, beneath the gloaming heaven of June,
   When peaceful rests the long voluptuous day,
   And but is heard the witching roundelay
That mavis sings to merle in sweetest tune,
We gaze upon its loopholed walls in pride—
Scotchmen have died for Scotland by the Clyde !

CATHCART CASTLE.

I LOVE to look upon its ivied breast
   When garish day has given place to night,
  When glows the golden moon, and sparkle bright
The old familiar stars in rich unrest,
And think of her who watched a battle-scene
   From the old tree which still is pointed out ;
   Who heard afar the combat's noise and shout,
And saw her banner fall—unhappy Queen !

When but the silent sound of aerial feet
 On the hushed ether greets my fancy's ear
 Mailed warriors and noble knights appear ;
A queen bewails her army's sore defeat ;
I see the anguish on her beauteous face ;
I bow my head as in a hallowed place.

DUMBARTON CASTLE.

O FOR a touch of old Æschylus' fire
 To sing this rugged rock and castle hoar !
 Æschylus, warrior-bard of buried yore,
Whose sword was ever ready as his lyre ;
Or for the sweeter strains Alcæus sang—
 Of swords at peace, in wreaths of myrtle dressed,
 When Liberty had given his people rest,
And o'er the land loud songs of freedom rang ;
For where could greater hero e'er be found
 Than Scotland's truest warrior, Wallace wight?
 Or where a nobler struggle for the right
Than that which made this castle hallow'd ground?
And where has Liberty a monument
Like these old walls, so sternly eloquent?

CRAIGNETHAN CASTLE (TILLIETUDLEM).

HIGH in the lofty ruined tower I lay
    On curious couch of immemorial moss,
    Watching below the tree-tops' gentle toss,
Breathing the balm of that blue summer day.
Looking along the level leafy lane,
    I thought upon the tale the wizard told
    Of those who came that way in days of old,
And fancy brought them to the scene again.
I saw the soldiers in their trappings gay,
    The Covenanters with their banner blue,
    The faithful servants and the lovers true,
The crowd returning from the popinjay.
O wondrous wizard power, that in our day
Makes people live who long have passed away !

LOCHRANZA CASTLE.

UPON the deck I stood in summer time,
    And saw the castle in the tinted bay
    Towering in all the grandeur of decay—
Hoar with long ages' crumbling, marring rime ;
A relic of the eras passed away
    When Scotland's kings resorted to its walls,
    When the whole island echoed to the calls
Of noble hunters riding all the day.

But where are now the lords and ladies gay?
   And where the glories of the Stuart race?
   Has earth forgot the valour and the grace
That filled these halls ere they were grim and gray?
Ah! names soon vanish in the ages long,
Save when the hero lives in poet's song.

SONNETS TO POETS.

REV. WILLIAM DUNLOP.

SONG is a sacred gift! sweet are the lays
    That take us back to childhood's happy hours,
    And sweet the lyre that sings of birds and flowers,
That of fair Nature's beauties sings the praise;
Sweet are the brave romaunts of buried yore—
    Of gallant deeds, of ladye, and of knight,
    That tell of those who fell in Freedom's fight,
And who are resting now—their warfare o'er;
But sweetest songs of all are they who sing
    Of Him who most deserves the lauding psalm;
    Such songs are fraught with joy and grateful balm
For human hearts downcast and sorrowing;
    Such songs are thine, O bard! and we admire
    The rich heart-throbbings of thy sacred lyre!

REV. FERGUS FERGUSON, M.A., D.D.

JUST as an acorn falling from the boughs,
  Takes root and springs up on the grassy lea,
  Growing betimes a giant-sheltering tree,
Within whose branches birds may find repose :
So precious thought, wrapped up in simple strain,
  May fall and sprout and ever greater grow,
  Filling sad hearts with glee and gladsome glow,
Giving them life, and light, and love again ;
" He lovèd me and gave Himself for me !"
  A saying ever old and ever new,
  Embalmed in song and long since dropped by you,
Has grown again as acorn to a tree ;
Weave on such golden threads of rhythm and rhyme,
And good will follow in the aftertime !

JOHN KELLY.

STRANGE-thoughted youth ! into my drooping heart
  Hath welled the summer music of thy song,
  As sunshine steals the shrunken flowers among,
Making the blossoms into beauty start.
Like thee, I love the summer's sunny hours,
  When Nature's minstrels hymn their holy mirth ;
  With thee I kneel when all thy soul goes forth
In worship to the beauty-tinted flowers.

May it be long ere life's deep griefs invade
   The rich heart-home where dwells such golden thought;
   Forever calm and peaceful be thy lot
Amid this life of changing " Light and Shade,"
And may the clouds of sorrow never roll
Across the sunlight of thy song-filled soul !

JAMES NICHOLSON,

AUTHOR OF " KILWUDDY; " " WANDERINGS IN THE GARDEN
OF THE SKY," &c.

DEAR Father Fernie (if a humble bard
   May tell thee how he loves thy doric lays
   Of humble village life in " langsyne " days,
So sweet and ne'er by affectation marred),
How dear to us thy songs !   They seem to bring
   The birds' sweet voice, the bees' unceasing hum ;
   And with the cadence of thy verses come
Kype's songful waters as they downward spring ;
How swiftly and how bright the moments fly
   When Father Fernie talks of leaves and flowers
   And who would care to count the passing hours
When " Wandering in the Garden of the Sky?"
The praise thy country gives thee thou hast won—
Of Scotland's sons of song a foremost son !

GEORGE MURIE, BELLSHILL.

CLOSE seated by the fire's bright, grateful blaze,
How often have we sat in winter-time,
Or pondered o'er some sweet and songful rhyme
Suggested by the summer's balmy days;
And sitting in my little room to-night
In the gray city I now call my home,
I picture thee beneath the azure dome,
Freed from the day's dull drudge and business fight;
Watching, perchance, the close of summer day
From Monkland Glen's deep shade of dusky trees,
Or straying thro' the gowan-sparkled leas
To " Roman Bridge" or grave of " Mary Rae;"
Ah ! friend, a greater boon there could not be
Than to possess the love of friends like thee !

WILLIAM HOGG.

WHY art thou silent, thou whose doric lyre
Erstwhile poured forth such wealth of joyous song
In praise of truth and right—dispraising wrong—
Sweeter to us than strains of classic fire?
With pleasure pure and unalloyed delight
Ofttimes we've read and lingered o'er thy lays,
When thou hast sung of summer's balmy days,
Or poured thy song unto the listening night.

What though no giant bard with thee returns,
   Dearer to us thy humble, homely strain,
   That frees the mourning heart from grief and pain,
In which the lyric fervour truly burns;
Then, still sing on.   The seeds you sow to-day
May bring forth fruit when years have rolled away !

JOHN MACDONALD (PANDORA).

TO thee, Pandora, and thy graceful lays,
   I raise these simple numbers, free from art;
   They are the true effusion of the heart,
And not the fawning flatterer's fulsome praise—
As such I know thou'lt prize them.   With delight
   I 've read the outpourings of thy soul refined—
   The dreamings of thy young poetic mind.
Oft in the solemn stillness of the night
   Have we twain strayed the city streets among,
Brooding o'er beauty and the hopes of youth—
Dreaming our dreams of life and light and truth—
   Cheering our hearts with scraps of starry song.
May thy life-journey lie 'mid pleasant ways,
To wake thy lyre to many joyous lays !

W. P. CRAWFORD.

("LEISURE LAYS.")

SWEET singer! often at the day's decline,
    Tired of those scenes in which I take a part,
    To soothe my weary brain and cheer my heart
I read and ponder o'er those "Lays" of thine.
Thy songs of Nature's birds, and trees, and flowers,
    Make me to feel the country's summer joys,
    And tho' among the city's cares and noise,
Thou bringest to my mind past happy hours.
Whether thou singest Ben-y-vrackie's praise,
    Or tellest the sad tale of "Mary Rae,"
    Or dreamest fondly o'er "Ye Eye of Day,"
The true poetic fire lives in thy "Lays."
Sing on, sweet singer, and thy honoured name
Will hold high place upon the roll of fame.

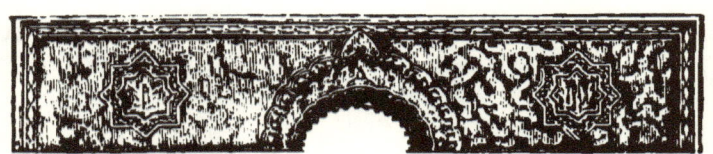

SONGS FROM THE FRENCH.

THE GUARDIAN ANGEL.

(BERANGER.)

TAE the puirshoose bed whar a wastrel lay
His guardian angel cam' ae day.
The puir saul cried in his misery:
"Don't tak' the trouble tae ca' on me—
 Ye've never dune ocht for me ava,
 Sae, guardian angel, heeste ye awa'!"

"Born in a garret, unheedit, unfed,
Wi' a battle o' strae ma only bed;"
"Thank me," quo' the angel, "for whit ye ha'e—
But for me ye wadnae ha'e haen that strae."
 "Ye've never dune ocht for me ava,
 Sae, guardian angel, heeste ye awa'!"

"Brocht up wi' mony a cuff an' fleg,
Turned adrift on the worl' tae beg;"

"Ay, but," quo' the angel, "I kep' you in rags,
An' wi' orra scraps I filled yer bags."
    "Ye've never dune ocht for me ava,
    Sae, guardian angel, heeste ye awa'!"

"Turnin' owre auld tae gang an' beg,
I listit, an' shortly I lost a leg;"
"I'm wae," quo' the angel, "tae hear ye rowte
That leg or this micht ha'e haen the gout."
    "Ye 've never dune ocht for me ava,
    Sae, guardian angel, heeste ye awa'!"

"Syne wi' the smugglers I wrocht a while—
My sole return wis a year in jile;"
Quo' the guardian angel : "Man alive !
Only for me ye'd hae gotten five."
    "Ye 've never dune ocht for me ava,
    Sae, guardian angel, heeste ye awa'!"

"Then, alack, I gat mairrit ae simmer day :
Ye 'll maybe claim credit for that job tae ?"
"I kent," quo' the angel, "o' your miscairriage :
But angels ha'e naething tae dae wi' mairriage."
    "Ye 've never dune ocht for me ava,
    Sae, guardian angel, heeste ye awa' !"

"Aweel, aweel, I 'm deein' noo ;
Whit prospects ha'e ye for me in view?"
Quo' the angel, "The prayers o' a priest, of course—
A coffin, a coach, an' a Belgian horse."

" Ye 've never dune ocht for me ava,
   Sae, guardian angel, heeste ye awa' !"

" An' efter that, is it laicher or higher?—
Streets o' gowd or a lake o' fire?"
" Ah ! there," quo' the angel, " my knowledge fails—
Suppose we toss for it, heids or tails?"
   " Ye 've never dune ocht for me ava,
      Sae, guardian angel, heeste ye awa' !"

The gangrel body kep' up the splore
Till a' the paupers war in a roar ;
Quo' the angel, " Frien', ere I depairt,
Confess I 've gi'en ye a lightsome he'rt."
   " Ye 've never dune ocht for me ava,
      Sae, guardian angel, heeste ye awa' !"

AN OLD MELODY.

(Nerval.)

THERE is an air I deem of sweeter tone
      Than music of Mozart,
An air that has a charm for me alone,
      Sad-sighing to my heart.

Whene'er that plaintive melody I hear
      The mists of ages flee—
Long centuries with swiftness disappear—
      An ancient scene I see.

A sunset shining o'er a castle's towers,
    And lighting up its halls ;
A river rolling on, 'mid smiling flowers,
    Laving the castle's walls ;

A face patrician, crowned with golden hair,
    Looks from a window high—
I feel that I have loved that lady fair
    In some age long gone by !

——

PROPHECIES.

(BÉRANGER.)

I'M posin', ma frien's, in a character new—
    Nae less than a prophet ye see in me noo :
If ye dinna believe whit I tell ye is true,
      E'en sae let it be !

The courtiers will ne'er think o' tellin' kings lees,
An' flattery an' fawnin' the great winna please ;
Puir poets will leeve jist like lords at their ease—
      E'en sae let it be !

Gamblin' in stocks will belang tae the past,
An' merchants be pleased wi' the cash they've amassed,
Ay, even their clerks will be ceevil at last—
      E'en sae let it be !

That queer kin' o' frien'ship will flourish nae mair
That passes awa' when a body turns puir,
But love shall reside in our he'rts evermair—
     E'en sae let it be!

Oor lassies will aye be fu' tidy an' clean,
An' never bring tears tae their auld mithers' e'en,
Nor think on the lads till they're "sweet eighteen"—
     E'en sae let it be!

Oor women will cast a' their pride tae the wa',
An' think no sae muckle o' aye dressin' braw;
Their husbands, nane feart, will can bide weeks awa'—
     E'en sae let it be!

Oor writers will fill their books fu' o' guid sense,
An' no tae a terrible wit mak' pretence;
They'll write for the richt, an' no for the pence—
     E'en sae let it be!

The authors will gi'e us a walth o' guid plays,
On actors wi' genius the audience will gaze,
An' even the critics will sometimes gi'e praise—
     E'en sae let it be!

If evil is dune by great men in that time,
We'll mak' it a jest an' we'll mak' it a rhyme,
An' fouk winna coont that a terrible crime—
     E'en sae let it be!

O' guid taste we'll ha'e a returnin' ance mair,
Oor judges' decisions will always be fair,
Oor puir fouk will never gae yammerin' sair—
  E'en sae let it be !

Eh? whit 's that ye ask ? "Kin'ly gi'e ye the date ?"
In the year twa thoosan' nine hunner an' eight !
No a meenit before, if we gang at this rate—
  E'en sae let it be !

THE BLACKSMITH.

(G. LEMOINE.)

THE smith his hammer swingin',
 Wi' a bang, bang, bang ;
Set a' the clachan ringin'
 Wi' his bang, bang, bang ;
 A buirdly loon wis he—
 An honest man and free,
 An' tae his hammer's clang
 A' day he sung this sang :
"Let lads wha lo'e the lasses sing their praises day by day,
Sic silly lilts jist show what little sense the fallows ha'e ;
The music I 'm maist fond o' is my honest hammer's ring,
Sae I 'll sing ma sturdy anvil an' ma hammer's praise I 'll
 sing."

Ae day the noise wis safter
　　O' the bang, bang, bang,
Nae echo shook the rafter
　　O' a bang, bang, bang,
　　For Mary's bonnie e'en
　　An' witchin', winnin' mien
　　Had changed the blacksmith's life,
　　An' noo she wis his wife !

"O strang and sturdy anvil, whase praise I 've sung sae
　　aft !
Ye 'll ha'e tae train yer lusty voice tae strains mair sweet
　　and saft ;
O true and trusty hammer! I 've lo'ed yer singing lang—
But through the wa' there wons a quean wha sings a
　　sweeter sang !"

Ae day there wis a racket,
　　An' a bang, bang, bang !
"Gin ye want a lickin', tak it !"
　　Then a bang, bang, bang !
　　The bodies fond o' clash,
　　Wha heard the lood stramash,
　　Gaed slinkin' canny by,
　　An' heard the blacksmith cry :

"O wife, O winsome Mary, doon at yer feet I kneel,
An' joyfu' is this he'rt o' mine yer wee white han' tae feel;
Nae leaf o' simmer roses tae my cheek could safter be—
An' if it pleases you, ma lass, it disna trouble me !"

THE BODY IN GREY.

(Beranger.)

THERE'S a cheery wee chappie that wons in yon toon
  Aye dressed in an auld suit o' grey;
Though sometimes he hasna a maik i' the warl'
  Ye'll aye fin' him happy an' gay.
      Ha! ha! ho! ho! he! he!
     I lauch an' I sing a' the day;
      Ha! ha! ho! ho! he! he!"
    Quo' the canty wee body in grey.

He smiles at ilk bonnie wee lassie he meets,
  At the "public" he rins up a score;
Up in debt owre the lugs, he is happy for a'
  Though beagles play tirl at the door.
    "Ha! ha!" &c.

He leeves in a garret up—gude kens hoo faur
  In the very worst pairt o' the toon;
In the winter the rain draps through on his bed,
  An' yet he is never cuist doon.
    "Ha! ha!" &c.

His wife has mair dresses than he could afford—
  Queer stories the neibors can tell—
An' tho' at the truth he has whiles a bit guess,
  He says na' a word tae hersel'.
    "Ha! ha!" &c.

When sometimes he's kept tae his bed wi' the gout
  The priest comes tae tell him o' grace,
Tae speak o' his sins an' o' death an' the deil—
  He leaves wi' a smile on his face.
        " Ha ! ha ! ho ! ho ! he ! he !
      I lauch an' I sing a' the day ;
        Ha ! ha ! ho ! ho ! he ! he !"
      Quo' the canty wee body in grey.

A HUMPH ON YER BACK.

[From the French.   Said to have been written by a rich but eccentric
  and deformed physician in Paris, and sung by him at a party
  to which he invited none but hunchbacks.]

THE cuif wad be only a puir doitit sumph,
    That wad chauner at fate for gi'ein' him a humph;
Punch and Judy, I'm sure, wi' the mob wadna tak'
Gin it werna that baith ha'e a humph tae their back !

The body wha thinks that a humph has nae use,
We may a' set him doon as a fule an' a guse ;
Should the win' blaw aboot ye, ye'll fin' for a fac'
That yer shouthers are lown wi' a humph on yer back.

A man may be clever, an' ne'er mak' a name ;
A man may ha'e wisdom, an' ne'er rise to fame ;
But the people's attention an' gaze ye'll no lack
If Nature has gi'en ye a humph on yer back.

" Oh ! weel wad I like tae ha'e walth o' gude gowd,
My simmer o' joy wad ken never a cloud,
I 'd big a great hoose, an' ilk room I wad pack
Wi' fouk that could brag o' a humph tae their back !

A statue I 'd ha'e in my gardens sae fine
O' Æsop, wha wrote in the days o' langsyne ;
Abune the front gate an inscription I 'd mak'—
" Success tae the man wi' a humph on his back ! "

THE EXILE.

(Lemennais.)

" One, a lone one, 'midst the throng !"—*Hemans.*

THE floo'rs are bonnie, the trees are green,
    But they seemna sae fair tae the weary e'en
That look in vain for the face o' a frien',
    An' the wanderer's he'rt is lanely !

The strangers are singin' the fiel's amang,
An' the strains are borne on the breeze alang ;
But oh ! for the lilt o' an auld hame-sang,
    For the wanderer's he'rt is lanely !

The wimplin' wee burns as saftly glide,
But they croonna sae sweet on a strange hillside
As they dae in the lan' whar fond memories bide,
    An' the wanderer's he'rt is lanely !

The faither sits wi' the bairn on his knee,
His sons a' roon' him—a sicht tae see—
But naebody here claims kin wi' me,
     An' the wanderer's he'rt is lanely!

It's oh! for the time when this life o' sin
Wi' a' its wae'll be past an' dune;
An' it's oh! for the rest o' the Hame abune,
     For the wanderer's he'rt is lanely!

"CARE, AWA'!"

DULL care, in yer wan'erin's hither and yon,
   Ye gi'e ilka body a ca',
Ye ha'e hung aboot me for a towmond or mair,
   But noo ye ha'e gi'en me a staw—
      Sae awa'!
  Ne'er again we'll forgaither, us twa!

When ye doitered aboot, wi' yer lang, m'urnfu' face,
   Ma chance o' enjoyment wis sma',
For yer sechin' an' sabbin' war aye at ma lug—
   In wud, or in dell, or in ha',
      But hurra'!
  Joy's bricht licht's beginnin' tae daw'!

If ever ye try tae come near me again,
   Wi' yer dour looks an' braith like the sna',
Ye'll get a begunk, for I'll keep ma he'rt licht,
   An' boo'na tae sorrow at a';
      Na! na! na!
  Sin' noo I hae got ye awa'!

THE KING O' YVETOT.

(BÉRANGER.   This song was suggested by the portrait of the king
above the inn-door at Yvetot.)

THERE ance wis a King o' Yvetot
    That history says but little o' ;
  His life wis free frae a' care an' dool,
  An' his croon wis nocht but a cotton cowl :
Wi' a ho ! ho ! ho ! an' a ha ! ha ! ha !
There was ne'er sic anither king, na ! na ! na !

Altho' his palace wis ruifed wi' thack,
O' guids an' gear he had nae lack,
  On a cuddy he rade aboot the yaird,
  An' a collie-dug wis his body-gaird !
Wi' a ho ! ho ! ho ! an' a ha ! ha ! ha !
There was ne'er sic anither king, na ! na ! na !

His royal spirits he ne'er let sink
As long as he 'd plenty to eat an' drink,
  An' a' the taxes that he wad ask
  War a half-a-gallon frae ilka cask ;
Wi' a ho ! ho ! ho ! an' a ha ! ha ! ha !
There was ne'er sic anither king, na ! na ! na !

He likit his men, an' they likit him,
An' were ready tae boo tae his ilka whim,
  An' it 's said he likit the lasses tae,
  An' that they wad his sma'est wish obey ;

S

Wi' a ho! ho! ho! an' a ha! ha! ha!
There was ne'er sic anither king, na! na! na!

Content wi' his inch, he ne'er wantit an ell;
His only law wis—" Enjoy yoursel' !"
    An' mony a saut, saut tear was shed
    Whan the auld king lay on his deein' bed ;
Wi' a ho! ho! ho! an' a ha! ha! ha!
There was ne'er sic anither king, na! na! na!

The gude king's picter still hings abune
The open door o' Yvetot Inn,
    An' there, at the fair-time, the rustics sing
    The sayin's an' dacin's o' their auld king;
Wi' a ho! ho! ho! an' a ha! ha! ha!
There wis ne'er sic anither king, na! na! na!

THE JOLLY BEGGARS.

(BERANGER.)

YE may sing o' love an' lasses,
    O' mountain an' o' dale ;
But I 'll sing the jolly beggars,
    O' canty fouk the wale.
        Sing hey ! the jolly beggars,
            Lang leeve they ;
            Huffy never,
            Frien'ly ever,
        Happy, blythe, an' gay !

If it's happiness ye're wantin',
  'Mang puir fouk ye maun gang ;
So says the Holy Scripter—
  So says ma canty sang.
    Sing hey! &c.

The maist contentit chappie
  In days o' auld langsyne,
Diogenes the Cynic—
  Leeved in a washin' byne !
    Sing hey! &c.

An' there wis furthy Homer,
  Wha trampt the hale day lang ;
An' nocht had he tae brag o'
  But an oak-stauf an' a sang.
    Sing hey! &c.

The rich fouk ha'e their troubles,
  Altho' they dress sae braw ;
The beggar's heid lies easy
  Upon a bed o' straw.
    Sing hey ! &c.

Whit tho' amang the gentry
  The beggar disnae move,
His he'rt is true an' kin'ly,
  An' fu' o' flowin' love.
    Sing hey ! &c.

The rich may tine their frien'ships,
 An' favours gi'en forget ;
But it 's no sae wi' the beggars—
 Na, na, frien's, oor side yet !
  Sing hey ! the jolly beggars,
   Lang leeve they ;
   Huffy never,
   Frien'ly ever,
  Happy, blythe, an' gay.

THE YEARS OF YOUTH.

OH, for the years of youth ! Oh, for the dear dead days !
 When I sorrowed not nor sighed, wandering in
  pleasant ways ;
Oh, for those joyful summers, dazzling with dreams of
 love,
Emerald around, beneath ; aerial azure above !

Lonely I linger now ; youth long has passed away :
Life is losing its music ; earth grows gloomy and gray :
But the green of the grassy meadows, and the creep of the
 crystal streams,
And the sweet, sweet spring of my life come to me oft
 in my dreams.

Feeble and failing and frail, I wearily wait for rest,

Longing to leave this life for the home of the happy and
blest ;

But still in my heart I 'll keep, till my soul from its cell
shall fly,

The gladsome greenness of youth and the memory of joys
gone by.

CUDDLE DOON.

CUDDLE doon, ma wean,
    A' sae warm an' cosy ;
Shut yer e'en again,
    Cuddle in a bosie.
Oh ! ma he'rt is sair
    Watchin' for yer daddie !
Will he come nae mair
    Tae his wife an' laddie?
      Cuddle doon, ma wean,
        A' sae warm an' cosy ;
      Shut yer e'en again,
        Cuddle in a bosie.

Will he ne'er come hame ?
    Noo his bairnie 's talkin',
Lispin' daddie's name,
    Roon' the kitchen walkin'.

He may come owre late—
    Oh ! the thocht is weary !
Oh ! the unco gate
    Owre the sea sae dreary !
Cuddle doon, ma wean,
    A' sae warm an' cosy ;
Shut yer e'en again,
    Cuddle in a bosie !

HERO ET LEANDRE.

DASHING high on the rocky ledge
    The Hellespont waters are foaming white,
Down where shivers the sheeted sedge
A lover stands by the water's edge,
    When the wind is sighing at dead of night.

"Soon will I see the maid of my dreams,
    Tho' the Hellespont waters are foaming white,
Bright from her window the clear light gleams,
To guide me o'er by its welcome beams."
    (The wind is sighing at dead of night.)

Hopeful he bravely leaves the shore—
    (The Hellespont waters are foaming white)—
But the light in the window gleams no more ;
The waves are leaping with sullen roar,
    And the wind is sighing at dead of night.

The stars in their silvery ranks arrayed,
    When the Hellespont waters are foaming white,
Look down and see in the turret's shade
A lover dead and a weeping maid,
    And the wind is sighing at dead of night.

A LASS I KEN.

(KING HENRY IV.)

SWEET the caller mornin',
    A' the east adornin',
Bonnier and sweeter faur a winsome lass I ken ;
    Sweet the simmer roses
    Whar sweet scent reposes,
Fairer faur her face than a' the roses in the glen.

    Sweet the birdies' singin',
    I' the wudlan' ringin',
But their sweeter liltin's frae ma lassie's lips are ta'en ;
    Sweet ilk blinkin' starnie,
    But compare they daurnae
Wi' the glancin' e'en o' ane I fain wad mak' ma ain !

OH, GIN I HAD A HUNNER HE'RTS.

OH! GIN I had a hunner h'erts,
    They'd beat for thee, they'd beat for thee;
  An' gin I had a hunner e'en,
      Thee only wad I see.
          Oh! ma bonnie lassie,
          Answer love's ae query—
          Can ye lo'e me, lassie?
          Will ye be ma dearie?
          Wantin' thee I weary,
          Life is dull an' dreary;
          Say ye lo'e me lassie—
          Mak' me gay an' cheery!
  Oh! gin I had a hunner tongues,
  They'd speak o' thee, they'd speak o' thee;
  An' gin I had a hunner han's,
    For you I'd toil wi' glee.

MY AULD BLUE COAT.

THE first day I wore ye fu' weel I can min'—
    My thretty-first birthday, it's ten years sin' syne;
An' nae maitter whit changes may fa' tae ma lot,
I never will tyne ye, ma auld blue coat!

'Though threadbare an' clootit an' fadit an' a',
Ye are dearer tae me than a coat passin' braw;
We ha'e braved mony storms, an' thegither we'll float
Doon life's stream a while yet, ma auld blue coat!

Ae nicht frae ma Leezie pretendin' tae rin,
She made clautch at ma sleeve, an' the claith bein' thin
It tore at the shouther; the place I aft note,
An' I lo'e ye for her sake, ma auld blue coat!

Nae dandified scents sprinkled owre ha'e ye ha'en,
Nor ribbons that cringin' and snokin' may gain,
Nor glaur, like the claes o' the wakeleggit sot,
Jist a flower at yer button, ma auld blue coat!

Some jokey fouk tell me I'll sune pass awa'
'Tae a climate whar coats arena needit ava'!
For sic' silly jokin' I carena a jot—
We'll pass life thegither, ma auld blue coat!

WHEN THOU ART AWAY.

(CHARLES D'ORLEANS.)

THINKING of thee ever, darling,
  All the weary day;
Wishing thou wert near me, darling,
  When thou art away.

What are earthly pleasures, darling,
    In their grand array,
When thou art not near me, darling—
    When thou art away?

All my cares and pleasures, darling,
    Thou alone can sway;
Thinking of thee ever, darling,
    When thou art away.

A DEAD BABE.

(VAUCELLE.)

NO more thou'lt play, sunned by thy mother's love—
    The love that cradled thee, that watched thee grow;
For death has called, sweet babe, and thou must go
To join the holy white-robed band above.

Dear little one! how short with us thy stay!
    But traces of thee linger in our home;
    Unto our hearts sweet thoughts of thee oft come,
And almost we forget thou art away!

TO A CRUCIFIX.

O SYMBOL, dear! gift of a dying hand!
 Her fading eyes were fondly fixed on thee,
Her latest breath thy ivory whiteness fanned,
  And dear thou art to me!

Chill with the breath of her last lingering sigh,
 Within my hands thou laid'st; and then my grief,
That till that time had mourned with tearless eye,
  In weeping found relief.

The torches threw their flickering light on high,
 The priest said solemn service for the dead,
In murmurs sweet as mother's lullaby
  Beside her baby's bed.

And there, white-robed, she lay; so calm her face,
 One could have thought she was not dead, but slept,
So beautiful, so sweet, so fraught with grace,
  What wonder that we wept?

Her marble brow shone in the fitful light
 Beneath her raven tresses disarrayed,
As we may see a mausoleum white
  Beneath the cypress shade.

One of her hands I fondly clasped in mine,
  The other lingered lightly on her breast,
As if it sought for thee, thou sacred sign!
    Where thou wert wont to rest.

The tree I planted o'er her grass-green grave
  Seven times has strewn its leaves around the spot;
But thou, the gift that she in dying gave,
    Since then hast left me not.

Worn next my heart, thou hast preserved to me
  The memory of her I loved so dear;
And there are traces on thy ivory
    Of many a bitter tear.

It was to thee her last request was sighed—
  A whisper soft that others could not hear;
Oh! tell me what she murmured ere she died
    To thee, thou image dear!

Ah! when we saw our loved one pass away,
  Grief closed our ears and gloomed our weeping eyes,
And swift her spirit left its home of clay,
    Deaf to our sobbing sighs.

In presence of the fell destroyer, death,
  Like full-ripe fruit upon the bending boughs,
Our souls hung trembling at each laboured breath,
    Waiting the mournful close.

Then, sacred symbol, cheer my drooping heart,
  And give my aching, anguished bosom rest ;
When she caressed thee, with her lips apart,
      What was her last request ?

Thou answerest not ! O dreary heart of mine !
  Thy tearful prayers, thy sighs, are all in vain :
But oh ! why should this cause thee to repine ?
      For we shall meet again !

Afar amid yon star-crowned heavenly throng
  She sees me here, and knows my heartfelt grief :
I seem to hear an echo of their song ;
      My heart finds sweet relief.

When 'tis my lot to cross death's swollen tide,
  I'll lay me down where last I clasped her hand,
And she shall come, my wandering soul to guide
      To the same Fatherland.

Oh ! when my soul is ushered into rest,
  May some true, tender friend be standing near,
To lay thee gently on my dying breast,
      Thou sacred symbol dear !

SONNETS FROM THE FRENCH.

IN EXILE.

(CHARLES D'ORLEANS.   Exiled in England for twenty-five years.)

WHERE castle-walls frown o'er the broad expanse
　　Of waving waters wailing all the day,
　I wander oft, and strain my eyes away
To where I know lies my own, long-loved France ;
The sea-birds flit across the waters blue,
　　Their white wings dripping with the snowy foam ;
　　Following their flight my eyes, in longing roam,
Wishing that I their passage could pursue.
Oh ! that their wings were mine, that I might fly
　　And reach my distant, happy France once more !
　　O Heaven, that I might gain its smiling shore,
Though it were but to lay me down and die.
One hour of love and liberty at home
Were more to me than weary years to come !

UNSPOKEN.

(Francis de Louvencourt de Vauchelles.)

THE time had come when I must needs depart,
　But, ah ! so swiftly sped the hours away
That I had found no time, no words, to say
To her the love that swelled my bursting heart.
I clasped her hand, but oh ! I did not dare
　To say " Marie, I love you !" lest a gaze
Should fill her eye of wonder and amaze,
Lest she should simply smile at my despair ;
And now, afar from her, I sit and sigh,
　And sigh again, to think that parting o'er ;
　O wingèd hours, now gone for evermore,
How sweet and swift that day ye passed us by !
Short-lived and bright as meteors that fly
Flashing an instant in the wintry sky !

"IF YOU CAN NUMBER."

(Joachim du Bellay.)

IF you can number all the gems that cling
　Upon the dusky brow of beauteous Night ;
If you can tell how many blossoms bright
Attend the coming of the smiling Spring ;

If you can say how many leaves shall fall,
  Brown-withered, in the sober autumn time ;
  If you can name, of every foreign clime,
Each jewel-cave and subterraneous hall ;
If you can count the sparks that upward soar
  From Etna's or Vesuvius' fiery caves ;
  If you can number all the rolling waves
That beat upon the rocky, lonely shore,—
Then you can tell the many virtues rare
Of her I love so well—my Olive fair !

TO OLIVE.

(JOACHIM DU BELLAY.)

GIVE back the charms that you have stolen away !
  Give to the gold the gleams that gild your head,
  Give to the rose your lips' enticing red,
And thy cheeks' ruddy glow to dawning day ;
Restore the love-light in your liquid eyes
  Unto the stars that glory gild the night,
  Unto the ivory thy soft hands white,
Unto the summer winds thy gentle sighs,
To the fair East your teeth of pearl belong,
  To little Cupid all your winning wiles,
  To statued Venus all your charms and smiles,
And to the skies your voice of sweetest song.
Thy name belongs to yonder leaf-clad tree—
And to the rock your heart—Ah me ! ah me !

IN THE NIGHT.

(TAHUREAU.)

'TWAS solemn night, the glistering, gleaming stars
   Glanced in the belt around the waist of night :
 The crescent moon, a ship of silv'ry light,
Dashed from her prow the foamy clouds' wave-bars.
Hushed was the din of day ; within each nest
   The feathered mother watched her sleeping brood.
   And I stood there, far in the silent wood,
With night's deep calm and peace within my breast.
Then came my love to me ; O golden spheres !
   O silver moon ! O nature soft asleep !
   Never a kiss so sweet—a joy so deep—
Or whisper sweeter to a lover's ears !
Dearer to me since then the night than day—
The night has given me happiness for aye !

THE LIGHT OF LOVE.

(RONSARD.)

ERE out of chaos came the slumbering light,
   A shroud of deepest darkness covered all ;
   Sunless and lifeless rolled the earth's dark ball,
And sea and sky were sunk in murky night.

9

So moved my soul within its night of clay,
  Until I saw the sunshine of your eyes ;
  Then woke my spirit in a glad surprise—
Then fled my night's nigrescent gloom away,
And I passed into gleeful joy and mirth,
  Into the beauty of a better life ;
  Soaring above the paltry noise and strife,
The wistful dreams, the soulless sounds of earth.
Erstwhile a thing without a stated goal—
A Being now : Love is my life—my soul !

DREAMS OF YOUTH.

(ANDRIEUX.)

O BRIGHT and blissful dreams of happy youth,
    How swiftly from our gaze ye pass away !
Sweet smiling youth—a sunny summer day—
How fraught with childish innocence and truth !
O happy time, when everything was bright,
  When to our eyes each object offered joy,
  Pleasure that cank'ring care could never cloy ;
When hearts knew naught of evil's clouding night.
The love of youth—can it no more return
  Unto the sad, world-weary, jaded heart ?
  Ah ! but the ashes into glow will start—
The flame no more will brightly, fiercely burn !
Alas ! these days can never be to me
Aught but an image and a memory !

IF IT IS LOVE.

(DESPORTES.)

I F it is love to roam with downcast eyes
   In lonely ways far from the homes of men,
  Whisp'ring myself, and whisp'ring back again,
Fanning the leaves and flowers with heartfelt sighs ;
If it is love to commune with the wind,
   To paint fantastic pictures on the air,
   To chide the night, and when the morning fair
Dawns in the east, to call the day unkind ;
If it is love oneself to cease to love,
   To feel forever longing and unrest,
   Then it is love that reigns within my breast,
That haunts me in the city and the grove ;
But neither pain nor prison could compel
My tongue the fervour of my love to tell !

PEACOCKS.

(GERMAIN PICARD.)

A PEACOCK wandered in a public park,
   Proud of his varied coat of feathery mail,
And, fan-like, spread his beauteous dazzling tail.
The people paused, his glowing tints to mark.

The bird was pleased, and to himself he said :
     " I shall be more successful if I sing,"
     And so he sang.   The effect was saddening—
The people gave not praise but blame instead.
So when a fop, well curled, well gloved, well dressed,
     Unto a social evening party goes,
     Fresh from the tailor's hands—a beau of beaux,
He causes a sensation ; and each guest
Admires his dainty figure as they pass ;
He speaks, they turn aside and say, " An ass !"

- -

A CHARACTER.

(CASIMIR PERTUS.)

HIS heart is full of envy, and a sneer
     Plays round his lips and glances from his eyes;
The men we look upon as good and wise,
He hates the more, the more we hold them dear.
A life devoted, loving, sweet, and calm,
     He in his dulness cannot understand ;
     The joys that only virtue can command,
He counts the dreamings in a world of sham.
When he can hurl a barbèd, venomed dart
     At aught of good, how proud, how pleased he is !
     But should kind thoughts like soft, sweet melodies
Steal thro' the darkened chamber of his heart—
Echoes of what had been in some far day—
Ah ! how he suffers till they pass away !

JUVENILIA.

THE WANDERER.

'THE night was dark and stormy,
    The moon refused her light,
The streets almost deserted—
    One form alone in sight;
And he was wand'ring slowly,
    With sorrowing, downcast air,
As if life were a burden
    Too hard for him to bear.
I tenderly approached him,
    And looked at him again;
I saw the signs of sorrow,
    The marks of heartfelt pain.
I asked him, in a whisper,
    What weighed upon his mind,—
If he, a lonely stranger,
    Had left his home behind.

Or if he wandered, brooding
O'er unrepented sins;
He murmured softly, sadly—
" Another pair of twins."

DEWS.

AS the sweet dew descendeth in the night
    And resteth on each plant, each branch, each leaf,
Giving the sun-parched foliage relief,
So that at morn they gleam forth fresh and bright,
Thus falls a gentle dew from Heaven above,
    When sorrow's night encompasseth the heart—
    When suff'ring causeth tears of pain to start—
The soothing, sacred, blissful dew of love.
Thus falls upon the soul the dew of faith,
    When o'er us steals temptation's murky night:
    It keeps us trusting in the coming light,
The morn that breaks beyond the gates of death.
    O dew of love, descend upon my breast;
    O dew of faith, upon my bosom rest.

LIGHTS AND VOICES.

WHEN on the earth our way is dark and drear,
    And we are languid with the world's hard fight,
When in the gloom of sorrow's dismal night
Our burdened hearts sink low with doubt and fear,

Then beams of light break through the clouded sky—
Love-lights to guide us to the land on high.
When, wearied with the trials of a day,
　　Our hearts are sick with hope so long deferred ;
　　When in our ear no friendly voice is heard
In loving tones to cheer us on our way,
A heavenly voice speaks to the doubting mind,
Bidding it leave earth's woes and cares behind.
　　O Light of lights, to me be ever near ;
　　O Voice of voices, linger in my ear.

ANOTHER ROAD.

A "HALLELUJAH Lassie" thought she'd try
　　To touch the conscience of a passer-by,
And waken in his breast some thought of heaven,
And thus she queried　"Sir, are you forgiven ?"
"*For Given ?*" quoth the man, and stopped to think :
"Naw, ah'm *for Partick*," and he wunk a wink.

"RUE IS IN PRIME."

A HUNDRED times I softly sighed
　　"Be mine, dear maid, be mine !"
Ere she consented.　Now I wish
　　I'd stopped at ninety-nine.

JOE BURGESS.

OUR junior clerk, Joe Burgess by name,
    Took a walk by the river along with his "flame;"
'Twas evening; the stars twinkled brightly above,
And Joe's bosom filled with romance, joy, and love.
"O darling," he cried, "by yon shimmering stars,
By the pale moon that sails thro' the silver cloud bars,
I swear that while this river rolls to the sea—
I swear that while life shall be granted to me—
I swear that as long as my name's Joseph Burgess,
I'll cherish thee, love, spite of Time's thaumaturges!"
"O Joseph," said she, "what grand words you speak—
How can you afford it on twelve bob a week?"

A DIRGE.

(*Memento Mori.*)

HERE lie those of every station—youth as well as
    age lie here;
Poor and lowly, high and mighty, priest and prophet,
    king and peer;
        Kind or cruel, evil, just—
        "Earth to earth and dust to dust."

Here lie men who fought and conquered, ne'er to
  join the battle more,
From life's turmoil now they're resting, all their
  earthly trials o'er ;
      Sword and shield have turned to rust -
      " Earth to earth and dust to dust."

Here the yielding and the valiant, weak and strong,
  alike are laid ;
Side by side the child and parent, hoary age and
  blushing maid ;
      These the grave will keep in trust—
      " Earth to earth and dust to dust."

Those who in their earthly journey felt temptation's
  dismal night,
Those who went through life undaunted, always
  battling for the right,
      Those who triumphed in their lust—
      " Earth to earth and dust to dust."

Cease, O heart, this sad repining ! Put away thy
  doubts and fears ;
There is One who sees our sorrow, One who wipes
  away all tears ;
      And, with faith in Him, we'll trust
      " Earth to earth and dust to dust."

MA NEW LUM HAT.

I FELL deep in love wi' a bonnie wee queen,
   Wi' cheeks red as roses an' bonnie blue e'en ;
An' tae mak' me look braw when we gaed for a chat
I spent a week's wage on a new lum hat.

Then ae Sunday nicht I wis dressed kinna douce,
I pat on ma lum hat tae gang doon tae her hoose ;
When I got tae the door, losh, ma fute took the mat,
An' awa' I gaed sprauchlin' the tap o' ma hat.

'Twis the auld man himsel' that had opened the door,
An' he kicked at ma hat, then burst intae a roar ;
" Preserve us," he lauched, " man, I thocht 'twis the cat,"
While I gloomily fondled ma new lum hat.

Hoo I wished for ma twa-skippet bannet jist then,
But ma troubles a' fled when ma lassie cam' ben ;
" Oh, hoo are ye, Tam ?—lay that doon, ye wee brat,"
'Twis her wee brither straikin' ma new lum hat.

We sat doon, an' oor chairs aye gat closer thegither,
Syne we baith sat on ane an' sent oot the wee brither—
Ye may lauch gin ye like, there wis naething in that—
'Twis tae hae a clear place for ma new lum hat.

We blethered awa' as fond lovers will blether.
Quo' I, " Dae ye no think we're haein gude weather ?"
Quo' she, wi' a smile, " Tam, I'm gled it's no wat—
'Twid ha'e wastit the nap o' yer new lum hat."

When the gloamin' wis fa'in' her mither cam' in,
Her sonsy big face lichtit up wi' a grin,
An' afore I could speak she composedly sat
Richt doon on the tap o' ma new lum hat.

"O woman, get up!" Quo' she, "Laddie, what's wrang!"
But I pushed her aside an' she fell wi' a bang,
An' there, on the chair, like a flounder as flat,
Wis a' that remained o' ma new lum hat.

I *fled*—but I dinna ken hoo I reached hame,
For I steekit ma e'en wi' vexation an' shame,
But I sat—an' I swat—an' I spat—an' I grat—
When the wreck I surveyed o' ma new lum hat.

But it ser'd as a lesson; in a' time to come
I'll ne'er play the dandy an' flourish a lum;
But ma temper's gey short, sae tak' care whit yer at—
An' never ance mention ma new lum hat!

SWEET VILLAGE MAID.

SWEET village maid, come roam the fields with me,
　　When from the earth night's curtain is withdrawn
　　When, in the glowing east awakes the dawn,
And ope the flowers on the grassy lea.

With softest strains of love the welkin rings,
  The butterfly and bee from flow'r to flow'r
  Flutter full early in the morning hour,
And far from earth the joyous skylark sings.
Brighter and brighter yet fair Phœbus glows,
  And lips of wild-flowers kiss the beauteous light,
  Sol's morning rays, so warm, refreshing, bright,
Open the eyelids of the dreaming rose;
But, 'midst them all, in garden, dell, or bower;
Sweet village maid, thou art the fairest flower!

APRIL.

WITH song of larks the joyous welkin rings,
  While all around, in woodland and in glen,
  Echoes the chirrup of chiff-chaff and wren,
And on the bank each lovely wild-flower springs;
The fields are covered o'er with daisies white,
  The hills are bright with cowslip and ox-eye,
  The buttercup and primrose woo the sky,
And all around gleam bluebells, azure bright;
All earth is lovely, pleasant to the sight,
  Since darksome winter now has passed away,
  And tho' made gloomy by the wintry day
We welcome back the flowers with delight;
So, when our hearts are dark with gloom and pain,
Then welcome April joys will come again.

LOVE'S SUMMER.

AS the sweet rosebud
    With tender hue
Wakes from its slumber,
    Kissed by the dew,
Modestly peeping
    At early morn ;
Thus wakes affection—
    Thus love is born.

And as the rosebud
    In summer hour,
Softly expanding,
    Becomes a flower,
Spreading sweet odours
    Through all the grove ;
Thus glows affection—
    Thus blossoms love.

But when the summer's
    Glad hour is fled,
The rose is withered —
    Its petals dead ;
So when affection
    Meets wintry skies,
Fond hearts will sever,
    And thus love dies.

AFTER LONGFELLOW.

(A Long Way.)

THE western sun was sinking fast,
　　As through the quiet street there passed
A tinker with a blackened eye,
Who ever and anon did cry—
　　　　　　"'Brellas to mend."

His brow was dark with smoke and soot,
His raiment, rags from head to foot;
And like a penny trumpet rung
The beery accents of his tongue—
　　　　　　"'Brellas to mend."

He lingered at the corner "pub,"
He drew his last coin from his fob;
He quaffed his glass of half-and-half,
And only answered, to their chaff—
　　　　　　"'Brellas to mend."

" Go not again," the landlord said,
" Wild blows the tempest overhead,
Your rags will lash you unto death."
Our friend replied with bated breath—
　　　　　　"'Brellas to mend."

" Oh, stay," the daughter said, "and rest
'Thy weary head upon this breast ;
Why should'st thou from our presence fly ? "
This was the tinker's sad reply—
                    "'Brellas to mend."

" Beware the stern blue-coated man—
Beware the falling chimney-can ; "
Such was the landlord's parting word,
And this was the reply they heard—
                    "'Brellas to mend."

In Duke street at the break of day,
Within a court the tinker lay ;
In falling he his leg had broke,
When gently raised, these words he spoke—
                    " 'Brellas to mend."

He died ; his body calmly rests ;
His ghost the lonely streets infests ;
And often at the midnight hour
A voice cries, with sepulchral power—
                    "'Brellas to mend."

A REMONSTRANCE.

(Nisi Dominus frustra.)

WEARY one, why let earth's sorrow
                    Fret thee so,
When thou knowest life is transient
                    Here below ?

In this life of grief and suff'ring,
                    Woe and pain,
Thou should'st always look above thee, —
                    Earth is vain.

When, dejected, thou art bending
                    'Neath the rod,
'Mid thy sadness and despairing,—
                    Look to God.

Uncomplaining bear thy burden
                    Through this life,
Heeding not the world's temptations,
                    Nor it's strife.

And thy sure reward will follow
                    When at last
O'er the earth sounds the Archangel's
                    Trumpet blast.

All earth's woes and weary strivings
        Shall be o'er ;
And thy heart shall sing with gladness
        Evermore.

SONNET—NATURE.

WHAT man could gaze upon sweet Nature's face—
    The pleasant vales, the little mountain rills,
    The craggy cliffs, the everlasting hills,
The little spring flowers with their laughing grace ;
Could stand alone in some dense pathless wood,
    Viewing o'erhead the green leaves' brilliant hue :
    Could watch the peaceful sky's majestic blue
From some green valley's glorious solitude ;
Could look upon the clouds that sail through heav'n ;
    Could feel the morning sun's refreshing rays ;
    Upon the gleaming stars of night could gaze ;
Or listen to the tempests wildly driven ;
Could look from earth below to heaven above,
And then deny a God of boundless love ?

SILENCE.

O'ER all the universe a wilderness
   Of silence reigned before the world began,
   Ere yet our God had fashioned beast or man,
A limitless expanse—a nothingness—
A silence vast, unbroken by the sound
   Of ocean's roar or voice of living thing ;
   Not e'en was heard the soft wind's whispering,
And all was changeless vacancy around.
But the Creator's word was sudden heard,
   And o'er the universe effulgent light
   Freed a pure, sinless earth from shrouding night,
And soon increasing man the green world shared.
But the stern trump shall sound, and once again
O'er all the universe shall silence reign.

CATS.

BENEATH his window the cats held concert,
   With a fervour and vehemence unsurpassed,
And his store of missiles—his boots and his slippers—
   Into the area were thrown at last ;
Then he spied a bottle of " Hair Restorer "
   And heaved it, sighing, "The *dye* is cast."

THE GOLDEN RULE.

YOUNG ladies, always kiss your friends,
    Your fathers and your mothers,—
Your nephews, nieces, uncles, aunts,—
    Your sisters and your brothers ;
So do, and you will always have
    The golden rule in view,—
" Doing to others as you would
    All men should do to you."

AN (UN)MUSICAL NEIGHBOUR.

I ONCE knew a man who was musical mad,
    A hundred years old was the fiddle he had ;
I never complained, but whenever he played
I wished he had lived when that fiddle was made.

PARODY ON "SUPPOSE A LITTLE COWSLIP."

SUPPOSE a little tin-tack
    Should stand upon its head,
And on some tempting easy-chair
    Uprear its point instead.

How swift the weary traveller
  Who sat thereon would start,
And with a malediction
  Caress the wounded part.

Suppose the little breezes
  Upon a winter's day
Should meet you at a corner
  And blow your "tile" away;
Would you not run and seize it,
  And press it on your "nob,"
Cut through some side street quickly
  And leave the jeering mob ?

Suppose the little toadstool,
  Half hid among the grass,
To some poor hungry traveller
  Should for a mushroom pass ;
Would not that little *fungi*
  Cause many a pang and ache,
And leave a train of suffering
  And sickness in its wake ?

GRIEF IS SHORT AND JOY IS LONG.

WHEN our hearts are wrung with anguish,
    When the hosts of sin are strong,
We should never be despondent,—
  Grief is short and joy is long.

When we pause and ponder sadly
 O'er some slight or fancied wrong,
In our hearts we should remember,—
 Grief is short and joy is long.

Tho' the floods of grief close round us,
 And we stand its deeps among,
Sorrow cannot last for ever,—
 Grief is short and joy is long.

Let us not be growing weary ;
 Tho' we are not always young,
Ever can our hearts be joyful,—
 Grief is short and joy is long.

Let our voices ring with gladness,
 This the burden of our song :
" Earth is dark, but heaven is glorious,—
 Grief is short and joy is long."

THE DEAD.

THE dust on which the living daily tread
 Is ashes of those who have trod this world,
But who by Fate's imperious hand were hurled
To join that mighty multitude—the dead.
" How are the mighty fallen " and passed away—
 Like ripples on the river they have passed,
 Or like the autumn leaves before the blast.

Where are the mighty ones who held their sway
O'er half the earth? The men of lofty state,
  Those who have left a never-dying name—
  Those whose good deeds have brought them glorious
    fame,
The priests and kings, the proud, the rich and great?
Ah! that dark river, with its ceaseless flow
And gloomy banks, forbids that we should know.

LIFE'S BATTLE.

HE who would overcome on life's stern field
    Must always ready be with sword and shield,
  And in the battle, difficult and long,
Must bravely stand to meet the coming foe;
And at the time appointed strike the blow
  With steady hand and heart both true and strong,
  For dark will be the conflict, and his life
Will oft be crossed with doubtings, strivings, fears;
And oft the eye will fill with bitter tears
  Before the end of this dark, bloody strife.
  Not for a day or year will last this fight,
But while life lasts the battle will be strong;
Some waging war and battling for the wrong,
  And others striving for the cause of right.

TIP-CAT.

A TIP-CAT,
  A wooden bat,
A happy little boy;
  A merry game,
  Eyes aflame,
Bosom full of joy.

  A tip-cat,
  A wooden bat,
A crash—a broken pane;
  A mother's knee,
  One—two—three—
" I'll never do't again !"

END OF THE CHAPTER.

HER head against his breast she placed;
    He wound his arms around her waist.
Thus he addressed the trembling maid—
" My loved one ! why art thou afraid?
Thy loving heart to me resign.
Fear not, but promise to be mine ;
Fly with me far across the sea—
A queen—an empress—thou shalt be !"

A heavy step sounds on the stair;
Opens the door, and on the pair
A stern and vengeful eye is fixed—
(*To be continued in our next.*)

LIFE'S LITTLE DAY.

CHILDHOOD is the morning
　　Of life's little day,
Dreamings are our dewdrops—
　　Hopes and fancies gay;
But as pass the dewdrops
　　From the flowery glade,
So our childish fancies
　　With the dayshine fade.

Working in the noontide,
　　'Neath the sun's warm darts,
All the dreamings vanish
　　From our weary hearts;
Ofttimes pass all pleasures
　　From our path away
In the busy noontide
　　Of life's little day.

Then when comes the gloaming,
　　And the shadows grey
Tell us of the closing
　　Of life's little day,

We will watch the sunshine
    Dying in the west,
Watching calmly, knowing
    Night will bring us rest.

THE WINTER WIND.

THE winter wind
    Blows strong and free
Over the land
And over the sea ;
'Thro' the tall trees
It storms and raves,
With wailing cry
It meets the waves,
And the bairns in the fisher's cot bend the knee
And pray for the breadwinners out on the sea.

    With gleeful hearts
    They'd left the shore
    In their little boats
    The night before ;
    But the boats go down
    And the tempest's breath
    Mingles with cries
    Of pain and death,
And the seamen are tossed, in cruel glee,
High on the waves of the storm-driven sea.

THE TRYSTIN' TREE.

THE sweetest spot to me, bonnie lassie, O !
　　Is aneath the trystin' tree, bonnie lassie, O !
　　　　The trystin' tree beside
　　　　The bonnie banks o' Clyde,
Wi' you close by my side, bonnie lassie, O !

Let misers hoard their dross, bonnie lassie, O !
Their pleasure's unco boss, bonnie lassie, O !
　　　　'Tis greater joy to me
　　　　Your rosy lips to pree
Aneath the trystin' tree, bonnie lassie, O !

The lordling's titled fair, bonnie lassie, O !
Could ne'er wi' thee compare, bonnie lassie, O !
　　　　Nae studied art or wile,
　　　　Nor ocht o' worldly guile,
Is seen in thy sweet smile, bonnie lassie, O !

Withoot thee I am sad, bonnie lassie, O !
When wi' thee I am glad, bonnie lassie, O !
　　　　Then come, my love, to me,
　　　　I'm waitin' here for thee,
Aneath the trystin' tree, bonnie lassie, O !

OLD MEMORIES.

I WANDERED thro' a shady country lane
   Where I had used to wander long ago,
And in the air I seemed to hear again
   The echoes of a voice I used to know ;
I seemed to feel a presence by my side,
   Altho' I knew that I was all alone :
   I seemed to feel a small hand in my own,
And, dreaming of the vanished past, I sighed,
For that sweet day-dream long had passed away
   The dream that brought my youthful spirit bliss,
   And passed away that voice, hand-clasp, and kiss.
Tho' backward still will memory oft stray ;
   And pain and pleasure mingle when arise
   From the heart's chambers these old memories.

A BEECH TREE IN WINTER.

I SAW this beech in the summer-time,
   When its leaves were lucent green ;
When the speckled mavis sang loud and clear
   O'er his home the branches between.

But leafless and songless now it stands
   When the winter tempests break ;
Like a ship dismantled by ocean storms
   That will soon be a hopeless wreck.

" Ah no ! with the tree that shall not be,"
   Cries the spring's prophetic voice.
" For soon again will its leaves be seen,
   And birds in its boughs rejoice."

"RATHER !"

A BARBER may lather
   His brother or father,
But if he'd be free from trouble and strife,
He mustn't attempt to " lather " his wife.

TIME *v.* MONEY.

A CREDITOR one day met
   Our fast acquaintance, Will ;
Said he, " Don't you think it's time
   You were paying that little bill ? "
Said Will, " Dear friend, your way
   Of putting the matter is funny—
Instead of a question of time,
   I think it's a question of money !"

AUGUSTUS GREEN.

AUGUSTUS GREEN was very "fast,"
    And used to smoke and drink and bet,
And all the neighbours whispered that
    Augustus Green was deep in debt :
So when at Brown's tea-fight he sang
    "Gently the *dues* are o'er me stealing,"
Each one that knew him smiled and said,
    " He sings it with a deal of feeling."

I WATCHED A ROSE.

I WATCHED a rose throughout the early spring,
    Blooming so beauteous,—blushing, balmy bright ;
But when I sought the flower but yesternight
I found it dead, a shrivelled, withered thing.
So short since 'twas the pride of all around —
    So delicately tinted—fair to see—
    Charming us with its matchless symmetry :
But now its withered petals strew'd the ground,
And ah ! this fate comes not to flowers alone,
    For earthly hopes, just bursting into bloom,
    Find, like the rose, full oft an early tomb ;
And often thus have sweetest day-dreams flown.
But ah ! how sweet the thought that far on high
There is a land whose flowerets never die.

"WEEPING MAY ENDURE FOR A NIGHT"
(Ps. xxx. 5.)

IT is not they who live a life of rest,
  Whose ways a peaceful, even tenor keep,
Who ne'er have source of pain or cause to weep,
That in this life alone are truly blest ;
For they whose eyes are ofttimes dimmed with tears
  Shall soon find sweet relief and smile again,
  And though their present lives be full of pain
A blessing comes to them with coming years.
Why should we weep for those who pass away ?
  Sighing and grief for earthly loss is vain ;
  Ah ! rather let us hope we'll meet again
In yonder happy land of endless day.
Dark grief may tarry through the troubled night,
But welcome joy shall come with morning's light

SWEET LASSIE O' LANGSIDE.

DOON by the bonnie banks o' Cart
  The sweet wee wild flooers spring,
An' in the lovely bluebell wud
  The blythe wee birdies sing ;

'Then in the gloamin' let us stroll,
  Whaur Nature's beauties bide,
Oh, meet me by the burnie's banks,
  Sweet lassie o' Langside.

Oh, what tae me are a' the joys
  That flooers an' birds can gi'e?
An' what the bonnie birdie's sang
  If thou art not wi' me?
Then let thy lovely presence cheer
  An' fill my heart wi' pride ;
Oh, meet me by the burnie's banks,
  Sweet lassie o' Langside.

THE AULD THACKIT BIGGIN'.

THERE'S a wee auld thackit biggin' that I aften gang
    an' see,
  It fills an unco corner o' my heart ;
Whaur at nichts we used tae gaither roon' a lovin' mother's
    knee,
  An' never thocht we'd ever ha'e tae pairt.
We'd listen tae her stories in the caunle's blinkin' licht,
  My faither noddin' in his auld airm chair,
Till bed-time cam' an' we were snugly happit for the nicht,
  In the wee auld thackit biggin' on the muir,
  The wee auld thackit biggin' on the muir.

But now it's cauld and cheerless, an' the win' blaws oot
    an' in,
    An' we are scattered far owre land an' sea,
An' some hae gane before me, frae this world o' dool
    an' sin,
    Frae a' life's cares an' sorrows they are free ;
But yet the thocht comes tae me that we'll maybe meet
    again,
    A thocht that cheers me when my heart is sair,
    For sadness aye comes owre me when my heart is
      backward ta'en
    Tae the wee auld thackit biggin' on the muir.

VOICES.

WHENCE come those whisp'ring voices, soft and low,
    That phantom-like at twilight hour awake?
Is 't from the golden sunset that they come
To haunt me with their far-off, dreamy tones?
They seem to speak to me of balmy spring,
Of summer with its sunshine and its flowers,
Of pensive autumn with its falling leaves,
Of merry winter and the falling snow ;
But ever, ever changing and far off
Those whisp'ring voices tell of long ago.

Whence come those tuneful voices at the dawn
That cheer me when my heart is filled with woe,

That seem to come ev'n from the gates of heaven?
They tell me of that distant "happy land,"
Its pearly gates and streets of purest gold;
They come to me like sound of golden harps;
And in the glowing east I seem to see
White, shining forms within the dazzling light
That beckon me.   And as they fade away
I know that night has passed and day is here.

—

FRIENDSHIP.

HOW few are faithful friends; how seldom met.
　　Friends unpretending, generous, and just,
　Friends in sincerity, friends we can trust,
And friends like these, when found, we ne'er forget.
　If such a friend is found in youthful years,
Who shares your mirth and misery, good and ill,
　　Who would not hurt your feelings even in jest,
Who in adversity shows friendship still,
　And all your sighing, all your sorrow shares,—
　　How deeply treasured in the grateful breast,
How well remembered by the thankful heart.
　Such friendship makes a calm of human life,
　And frees us from a load of care and strife,
And sad the hour when friends like these depart.

HEROES.

AH ! there are heroes in this world of ours—
    Unlike the heroes who in battle fell ;
  Heroes who fight, and strive, and battle well,
Not with their fellowmen, but with the powers
Of evil and oppression.   O'er our land
    Stalk these gaunt giants, with their poison breath,
    Spreading around them want, disease, and death ;
O'er torn hearts treading like an armed band,
Rejoicing when they see the hot tears start,
Rejoicing when they cause a broken heart,
    Striking alike at feeble age or youth,
    Sworn enemies to chastity and truth ;
But we have heroes, men of real worth,
Who 'll strive to drive such giants from our earth.

MARTYRS.

'TIS not alone those who were bound in chains
    And tortured till death came to end their pains,
Nor those who in the fight for freedom fell,
That the great list of this earth's martyrs swell ;
For there are martyrs to the world unknown,
    Who all their sorrows bury in their breast,
    To whom death comes not with the longed-for rest ;
And yet the world has never heard them groan.

Martyrs whose lives are one long silent grief,
  Whose every day is full of doubts and tears,
  Whose every hour is fraught with woes and fears,
Who daily pray for death to bring relief;
  And death alone will bring their souls release,
  And give their wearied spirits lasting peace.

THE RACE FOR WEALTH.

"PAPA, what is meant by the race for wealth?"
  Cried little Johnnie, with eager face;
And the father abstractedly answered the boy,
  "The race for wealth is the Jewish race!"

"HOME, SWEET HOME."

SAWTAN i' the law court
    Wis ance, sae I 've heard tell—
"Oh! but hame is hamely!"
    Quo' Sawtan tae himsel'.

DOCTOR OF DIVINITY.

A REVEREND doctor sat with a friend,
    "I play on the violin, sir," said he;
And his friend, who wasn't a musical man,
    Impatiently muttered, "O fiddle D.D.!"

SHE WAVED IT WILDLY.

SHE waved her hand wildly to stop the car,
    But, instead of at once obeying,
The tramway guard smilingly sang to himself
    " What are those wild waves saying?"

STORM VISIONS.

OVER the stirful city the storm-wind roars and raves,
    Like the dying shriek of drowning men 'mid the
        rush of ruffling waves,
Like the sorrowful wail of a restless ghost moaning at
    midnight hour,
Through the secret chambers and silent halls of some
    lone ruined tower ;
And pictures rise before my mind of a mountain lone
    and drear,
And a weary traveller staggering on, o'ercome with
    cold and fear ;
Of a forest bending and roaring—-of a dreary and wild
    morass ;
Of snow-wreaths whirling madly in a rugged mountain
    pass,
And stark and stiff on the white hillside a figure I seem
    to see,
While the wanton wind laughs weird and wild in
    demoniac jubilee.

I see the gravid gray green waves rise from the wildered
    sea—

Rising with rapid rasping rush, groaning in ghoulish glee;

I see the parting-timbered ship driven by the east
    death-wind—

I see the bold crew lower the boats, I hear the grapnels'
    grind ;

Higher the billows rise from the vast—louder the storm
    fiends laugh—

And the graceful ship with its gracile spars sinks in the
    murky graff.

Curling and swirling the waves roll on, climbing the
    clustering rocks,

That will soon be covered with spar and rack torn by
    the tempest-shocks.

O Thou, who stilled the tempest on the Lake of Galilee,

To Thee we pray to watch o'er those in danger on the sea.

CAWTHOR WATER.

HOO bonnie is the ripplin' stream,
    As 'neath the sun's refreshin' beam,
Aroon' the Holm, wi' brichtsome gleam,
    Flows bonnie Cawthor Water.

Here brichtest bloom the flooers in spring,
An' blythe wee birds the loodest sing :
Whaur giant oaks their shadows fling
    Owre bonnie Cawthor Water.

Here saftest blaws the summer breeze
Amang the stately, dark fir trees,
An' loodest hum the summer bees
    By bonnie Cawthor Water.

An' when the Autumn breezes blaw
An' gowden leaves begin tae fa',
'Tis still the sweetest spot o' a'—
    By bonnie Cawthor Water.

Ay! ev'n when winter's frost an' snaw
Wi' spotless mantle cover a',
I love to rove, tho' cauld win's blaw,
    By bonnie Cawthor Water.

Ye ask me why I sing its praise,
An' on its waters fondly gaze?
Ah! freen', I spent life's early days
    Near bonnie Cawthor Water.

An' when wi' glee we left the schuill,
An' roamed the country roon' at will;
Oor wearied limbs we'd aye tae cuil
    In bonnie Cawthor Water.

'Twis then I met wi' frien's sincere,
Whose memories I 've cherished dear;
An' mony a time we wan'ered here
    By bonnie Cawthor Water.

At hame, in yon'er noisy toon,
Wi' nocht but streets an' lanes aroon',
I often long tae hear the soon'
   O' bonnie Cawthor Water.

Tho' severed far by dale an' hill,
In dreams I seem tae see it still—
The hie auld brig, the ruined mill,
   An' bonnie Cawthor Water.

Tho' those bricht happy days are o'er,
An' youth has fled for evermore,
I lo'e it as in days o' yore—
   The bonnie Cawthor Water.

A CHRISTMAS CAROL.

LONG ago, 'mid heavenly music,
   Came to earth the angels fair;
Spake unto the wand'ring shepherds
   The glad tidings which they bare.

Told them how, within a manger,
   He, the new-born Saviour, lay;
Born on earth to seek for sinners,
   As their life, their truth, their way.

And when comes this joyous season,
   In our hearts we hear again
Echoes of the heavenly chorus;
   "Peace on earth, goodwill to men."

Then let us be ever joyful,
  Banish sorrow from our homes ;
Let our cares be all forgotten
  When the " Merry Christmas" comes.

For although the lapse of ages
  Lies between us and that morn,
Ev'ry Christmas-tide He cometh
  To our spirits newly born.

Tho' exalted now He reigneth
  In a glory His alone—
Circled by a light eternal,
  Sitting on His heavenly throne,

Still His heart yearns for the wand'rers,
  Still for man His pity bleeds ;
And with those who yet despise Him,
  Oft His Holy Spirit pleads.

Let us then still spread the message
  Brought us by the angel band;
Spread it over hill and valley,
  Over sea, and over land.

Send it to the darkest desert—
  To the islands of the main—
Spread it o'er the whole creation,
  " Peace on earth, goodwill to men."

"I WILL BOTH LAY ME DOWN IN PEACE, AND SLEEP."—Psalm iv. 8.

WHAT though the world around me fret and frown,
   What though death's shadows thickly o'er me
      creep,
Without one thought of dread, one dream of care,
   "I will both lay me down in peace, and sleep."

Not the gay landscape, nor the glorious sun
   Could e'er assuage the woes of those who weep ;
But He will wipe away all tears, and so
   "I will both lay me down in peace, and sleep."

When all the earth is silent in the night,
   He sends His guardian angels watch to keep,
And though the winter's storms around me rage,
   "I will both lay me down in peace, and sleep."

And when the cares and woes of life are o'er,
   And death brings slumber peaceful, dreamless, deep,
He will provide a haven of rest for me—
   "I will both lay me down in peace, and sleep."

THE DEATH OF DOUGLAS.

[The spirit of romantic adventure inspired him (Bruce) to the last, and he desired his faithful follower, Sir James Douglas, to carry his heart to the holy sepulchre at Jerusalem. That worthy knight considered the dying bequest more imperative than the commands of his living sovereign, and he conveyed the heart in a silver casket through difficulties and dangers, until he was killed in Spain in battle with the Saracens, after having thrown the casket before him, saying—" Onward, as thou wert wont, brave heart! Douglas will follow thee!"— *White's History of Scotland.*]

HE stood amid his turbaned foes, and gazed on
Bruce's heart,
A relic of the olden days with which he would not part :
He saw the warlike Moorish lines in sullen anger stand,
And fiercely closed his fingers on his faithful Scottish
brand ;
He thought of bonnie Scotland, the land to him so dear,
A distant sounding pibroch seemed to fall upon his ear;
He thought upon those vanished days of changing war
and truce,
Of his old northern comrades, of his monarch—Robert
Bruce,
Of Edward's fierce oppressions that made poor old
Scotland mourn,
And of the glorious victory on storied Bannockburn.
Beneath his gleaming breastplate his bosom rose and fell,
He gazed upon the faithful few who followed him so well ;

Then flinging forth the Bruce's heart, he cried, in accents
    free :
" Onward, as thou wert won't, brave heart ! Douglas will
    follow thee !"
Loud o'er that dreadful field of blood his battle-cry arose,
As with his broadsword in his hand he charged his dusky
    foes ;
The turbaned foemen round him swarmed like storm-
    waves on the shore,
And soon the gallant Scottish warrior fell to rise no more ;
And when his followers gained the spot where he had
    passed to rest,
They found the heart of Robert Bruce close clasped to
    Douglas' breast.

—

TO MY FRIEND JOHN ALEXANDER.

[In answer to his poems in *Glasgow Weekly Mail*, entitled " Prood
  Fortune's ta'en a spite at me," " I tried tae wade misfortune's tide,"
  " The puir man's road lies up a brae," &c.]

THIS life is but short, an' we 'll sune pass awa',
    Then why should we fash aboot trouble an' care ?
Altho' doon the brae, we should never despond—
    A fig for misfortune, Jock, " Never despair !"

The cup o' contentment is aye at oor han',
    Then why should enjoyments and pleasures be rare ?
Come, drink o' its nectar, 'twill 'liven ye up—
    A fig for misfortune, Jock, " Never despair !"

When fechtin' alang 'mid the battle o' life
    Misfortunes ye'll meet wi', but them ye maun dare;
Aye cairry before ye the bricht shield o' Hope—
    A fig for misfortune, Jock, "Never despair!"

Man, warfare has aye a weird charm o' its ain,
    An' Vict'ry rewards for the ills ye've tae bear;
Gang intil't wi' spirit—for Victory strike—
    A fig for misfortune, Jock, "Never despair!"

But, Jock, lad, tak' tent that ye strike for the richt,
    An' ye'll reap the reward when on earth ye're naemair;
Aye strike for the richt, an' be never cast doon—
    A fig for misfortune, Jock, "Never despair!"

REST.

'TIS what we ofttimes sigh for in this life,
    The hour of rest, when we can view the past
Safe from each wintry storm—each howling blast;
Rest from the world's annoyances and strife.
"Oh! where can rest be found?" Not with the great,
    The vaunting owners of an ancient name:
    Not in men's praises, or a world-wide fame;
Not ev'n on nation's thrones 'mid kingly state.
Childhood, nor youth, nor manhood, nor old age,
    Secures for us the balmy quiet of rest.
    He who has found it, happy is and blessed,
Regardless of life's tempests, calm and sage.
    'Tis in the humble mind   the virtuous breast—
    Where may be found peace, trust, and blissful rest.

MERCY.

HOW welcome must the news of mercy be
    To those who have transgressed, and guilty stand ;
  How gladly they will grasp the giver's hand,
And, thankful, bend to him the willing knee.
All we who now upon this dark earth live
    Have sinned beyond our knowing, and our debt
    Is noted.   Great are our transgressions. yet
Our Creditor will willingly forgive
Whene'er we feel our utter poverty.
    'Tis only when we know that we are poor,
    That He in mercy grants to us a cure.
And sets our burdened, guilty spirits free.
    His mercy is for ever one ordained ;
    " The quality of mercy is not strained."

OH, THINK OF ME, LOVE.

OH, think of me, love, when I shall be dwelling
    Far from my home, o'er the boundless blue sea ;
When the wild waves in their anger are swelling,
    Oh, think of me, love, think only of me.
When o'er the spring-flowers the sunbeams are shining,
    Happiness bringing to bird and to bee,
When you are watching the sunset declining,
    Oh, think of me, love, think only of me.

Oh, think of me, love, when I shall be dwelling
    Far from my home, o'er the boundless blue sea;
When the wild waves in their anger are swelling,
    Oh, think of me, love, think only of me.

When, o'er the dark earth, the bright stars are keeping
    Watch till the dreary night-shadows shall flee;
When, in the night, on your pillow you're sleeping,
    Oh, think of me, love, think only of me.
Whether in sorrow thou art or in gladness,
    Living in pain or surrounded by glee,
Whether thy spirit knows pleasure or sadness,
    Oh, think of me, love, think only of me.

Ever to thee shall my fond heart be turning,
    Ever my thoughts to my loved one shall flee,
Ever for thee shall my spirit be yearning,
    Oh, think of me, love, think only of me.
If one should tell thee thy lover is faithless,
    Heed him not,—faithful to you I will be;
Darling, my love shall be lasting and deathless,
    Oh, think of me, love, think only of me.

———

LIFE.

WHAT is life?
    A fleeting vision,
Just a dream and nothing more:
Just a dream that soon will vanish
Ere we reach the other shore.
    A fleeting vision—
      Such is life.

What is life?
    A heaving billow,
That but one short moment stays,
Then, returning to the ocean,
Never more will meet the gaze.
    A heaving billow—
      Such is life.

What is life!
    A beauteous blossom,
Glowing on a summer's day,
Scenting all the dewy meadow,
Then swift falling to decay.
    A beauteous blossom—
      Such is life.

What is life ?
A passing journey,
Sometimes marred by earthly strife ;
Death is but the gloomy portal,
Leading to eternal life.
A passing journey—
Such is life.

SING TO ME.

MOTHER, sing to me again—
Sing to cheer my aching heart :
Let me hear thy voice once more
Ere my spirit shall depart.

Mother, sing to me again—
Let me lean upon thy breast,
And, as in my youthful days,
Sing thy wayward child to rest.

Mother, sing to me again—
Say you still your wand'rer love ;
For the heart once hard and cold
Now is fixed on things above.

Mother, sing to me again—
Kiss me as in days of yore ;
Murmur not, I go to join
The angels on a better shore.

FORGET-ME-NOT.

WHEN, broken hearted,
    Last night we parted,
You gave to me a sweet forget-me-not;
    Ah! love, believe me,
    I'll ne'er deceive thee,
Ne'er shalt thou be by this fond heart forgot.

    Forget thee? Never!
    Till death us sever.
And from this earth my soul with gladness flies;
    I'll thee remember
    Till life's last ember
Dies here to kindle brighter in the skies.

THE VETERAN.

WHEN a passing rumour goes over the country
    Of war's alarms,
'This is the cry of the one-armed soldier,
    "Two arms! two arms!"

OBITUARY.

"DOWN the line I 'll go," he said,
　　To reach the railway station.
Friends will please accept of this
　　(*The only*) *intimation.*

—

SMITH.

WITH 'buses and cars and lorries and carts
　　The street was full of noise,
The various schools poured forth their troops
　　Of loud-voiced girls and boys ;
The landlady's voice, in furious tones,
　　Was echoing through the "land ;"
Just under the window loudly played
　　A discordant German band ;
And Smith, the boarder, murmured low,
　　"Man wants but little *'ear* below."

GOOD-NIGHT.

THE sun has set—o'er all the earth
　　The pale moon throws her light :
The evening bird swells forth its song—
　　Good-night, my love, good-night.

May those sweet eyes of heavenly blue
  (The stars themselves less bright)
Be closed in peaceful, quiet sleep—
  Good-night, my love, good-night.

Sweet be thy dreams; no visions dread
  Intrude upon thy sight,
But peace and joy upon thee rest—
  Good-night, my love, good-night.

CITY ARABS.

ONCE they were innocent, undefiled,
    Children that gleefully played and smiled ;
But, nursed in those direful dens of sin—
Accustomed to oaths and drunken din—
What will they be in the coming time
But masters in guilt, adepts in crime ?
Can we not save them from sin and scorn,
Change the night of their lives to golden morn,
Save from the drink fiend's terrible curse—
Save the boys from crime, the girls from worse?

If allowed to tread this unwholesome soil
With never a teaching of honest toil,
With never a knowing of wrong from right,
They will sink to deadlier depths of night:

Bearing, perchance, the felon's name—
Bearing for ever the brand of shame.
Then bring them in from the stirful street,
Where they live in hate or die 'mong our feet,
From the haunts of want and crime and sin,
Unheeded jewels, oh! bring them in.

--- ---

TO CORRESPONDENTS.

SING! poets, of the summer flowers and trees,
 Send us your rhymes as soon as e'er you can, sirs;
Write only on one side the paper, please—
 We need the other side for writing answers.

"TWO SOULS WITH BUT A SINGLE THOUGHT."

 " MY soul is at the gate!"
  The sighing lover said;
 He wound his arms around her form,
  And kissed her gold-wreathed head.

 " My *sole* is at the gate!"
  The maiden's father said:
 The lover rubbed the smitten part,
  And from the garden fled.

ROOM FOR ONE.

JOHN JONES was old and very stout,
  (To him this was no fun),
And just the omnibus back stair
  To climb he had begun,
When waggish Smith cried out—" Keep back,
  There's only room for one."

—

LOST YOUTH.

COULD I but live again those years
  When fancy wayward ranged,
How different would each action be—
  My way of life how changed.

Could I but those past years recall,
  Earth's pleasures I would pass ;
I'd choose that better way in which
  None ever sigh " Alas !"

But ah ! the longing is in vain,
  Those youthful days are gone :
And Time, unchangeable and stern,
  Is ever marching on.

My heart, if time I could erase,
　　Might, as of old, soon stray,
And from the path of rectitude
　　Wander far away.

So I will struggle to forget
　　The errors of the past,
Hoping for better days to come,
　　And happiness at last.

BARBAROUS.

'TWAS a cheap barber's shop an' the razor wis dull,
　　An' tae get the beard aff took a geyan hard pull :
The victim cried oot, wi' his mooth fu' o' saip ;
"I doot I 've got intae an unco bad *scrape !*"

———

TOMPKINS.

AS Tompkins bears his first-born
　　Down the nursery stair,
　　　The baby cries,
　　　And Tompkins sighs—
"There 's music in the *heir !*"

OLD JOHN.

" I CAN'T *find* bread for my family,"
    Said old John's thriftless neighbour ;
" Nor I," said old John, " I 've to work for it,
    And ne'er got it yet without labour."

MICHAEL FLYNN.

SAID Michael Flynn, the labouring man,
    " Yis, sorr, although oi'm poor,
Sooner than live on charity,
    Oi'd beg from dhure to dhure !"

A PRAYER.

LIFE is fraught with tears and sighing,
    Grieving, hoping for the best ;
But do Thou, in grace complying,
    Send, oh send us rest.

By the darkness sore confounded,
    How we dread the dreary night,
But Thou art by light surrounded
    Send, oh send us light.

Much Thy cheering help we 're needing,
  Earthly pleasures quickly cloy;
Thou, who hearest all our pleading,
  Send, oh send us joy.

Often to the world returning
  How our wayward footsteps rove;
Thou, who art for wand'rers yearning,
  Send, oh send us love.

Day by day our foes distress us,
  And our enemies increase :
Thou, who canst from all release us,
  Send, oh send us peace.

When we leave this dark earth's sadness—
  Pass away from care and strife—
Thou who reign'st mid joy and gladness,
  Send, oh send us life.

I SAW HER BUT A MOMENT.

I SAW her but a moment
    Beneath the apple tree,
There was no one to listen;
    No eyes were there to see;

I heard her soft voice singing,
  Her song was one of love,
Her bright eyes seemed to borrow
  Light from the stars above.
I saw her but a moment
  As 'neath the tree she sat ;
I at her threw the poker—
  (She was—my neighbour's cat.)

THE CAUSE.

BENEATH the wave lies the gallant skipper
  Of the " Nancy " clipper.
The cause of his death is stated concisely —
" He *luffed* not wisely."

NO HARM DONE.

" KEEP off that wet dado," shouted the painter.
  "How often, you fool, will you have to be told?"
"Oh, never mind," said the careless apprentice,
  " It doesn't matter, *my clothes are old!*"

CHILDREN'S VOICES.

ALL music is sweet to my ear, but the sound
  At which my fond heart most rejoices,
Is the music of sweet little children at play,
  And the glee of their merry young voices.

Let some seek amusement in this thing or that ;
  As a source of pure pleasure my choice is
To gaze on the antics of children at play,
  And list to the sound of their voices.

Wherever are gathered the sweet little girls,
  And wherever the game of the boys is,
There is always a lesson for elders to learn,
  And joy to be found in their voices.

Though cankered old neighbours may pop out their heads
  And ask what that horrible noise is?
Let them fret as they like, there are many who bless
  The sound of the children's voices.

TO THE ROMAN BRIDGE

Over the South Calder Water, near Bellshill.

WHAT mem'ries of the olden time dost thou recall,
  old Arch !
An ancient monument thou art of Rome's triumphal
  march,

For over thee Agricola's and Adrian's armies vast.
And Urbicus the Conq'ror with his warlike legions passed ;
And thou hast seen the native chief, Galgacus, put to
flight,
And then upreared thy rugged head through centuries of
night ;
Perchance thy hoary summit St. Columba may have
paced,
When with his holy mission he our savage Islands graced.

A silent witness thou hast been of struggles for the right,
A witness of the injuries and wrongs of Wallace wight,
A witness of the struggles of our hero, Robert Bruce,
Who taught the Southron foemen that they shouldna
craw sae crouse,
And good Lord James of Douglas has often made thee
ring
When leading on his followers to aid their lord the King ;
Thou may'st have heard the Scottish hearts that swore
"tae dae or dee,"
With Murray's name and Randolph's fame familiar thou
must be,
And thou hast seen those noble heroes fighting pass
away,
But the freedom that they struggled for (and gained) is
ours to-day.

If thou had'st but the power of speech, what stories thou
could'st tell
About the martyr'd heroes in religion's cause who fell—

Of the Covenanters' trials, of their troubles and their ills—
Of their worshipping in secret, of their meetings 'mongst
the hills,
Of the cry to God for succour, of the broken spirits' wail—
Of Warriston, of Guthrie, of sainted Hugh M'Kail—
Of brave Argyle, of Balfour, who for freedom fought and
bled,
When Claverhouse and stern Dalziel their savage minions
led ;
But the faithful were triumphant, for they conquered when
they fought,
And we now enjoy the freedom their devoted blood has
bought.

What changes thou hast seen around, what dynasties
o'erthrown,
The dying patriot thou hast seen, hast heard the martyr's
moan :
When civil war around thee raged and families were
estranged,
What changes thou hast witnessed and yet remained
unchanged :
And still in future years thou may'st uplift thy rugged
head,
When generations yet to come are numbered with the
dead.

MARY RAE.

ALONG the banks of winding Ayr
    There roamed a loving youthful pair :
She was a maiden bright and fair.
With glorious wealth of golden hair :
Her brilliant eyes of deepest blue,
Her lips of the vermilion hue ;
Sweet as the blossoms of the May.
The village belle was Mary Rae—
A gentle, winning, queenly maid,
Though but in plain attire arrayed.
He was a brave and gallant youth,
Whose every feature beamed with truth,
Whose manly form did not belie
The soul that shone forth from his eye ;
But pale and pensive was his cheek—
His heart so full he scarce could speak :
And she, the one to him so dear,
Could scarce repress the rising tear,
For Robin Lambie must depart
To take in freedom's fight a part :
Must go to join the faithful few
Who to the Covenant stand true—
Who, for their Gospel and their faith,
Would brave e'en martyrdom or death.
No wonder Robin oft should sigh,
No wonder tears dim Mary's eye,

And that their parting they should mourn,
For he may ne'er again return ;
But Robin strove to calm her fears,
He kissed away her rising tears,
And thus he spoke : " My Mary, why
Should parting make us grieve and sigh ?
'Tis for the truth I go to fight,
And right will surely conquer might—
Our martyrs' blood cries from the dust,
And in *their* God we put our trust."
But Mary's bosom rose and fell
(Poor lass, she loved her Robin well),
And paled her cheek, as soft she said :
" Last night, while sleeping on my bed,
At midnight hour I had a dream :—
I saw a broad, swift-rushing stream
With armed men on either ridge,
And foemen crowding o'er a bridge ;
I then beheld a fearful fight,
Followed by victory—and *flight*.
O'er all the field lay weapons red,
The river's banks were strewed with dead—
And in one livid, ghastly face
I could my Robin's features trace."
But Robin said : "I trust in One
Who doeth right—His will be done !"
And soon to join his friends departed—
Leaving poor Mary broken-hearted.

Bright shone the summer sunshine o'er
Old Bothwell Castle's ruined tower :

The sunbeams, laughing, seemed to glide
Along the fir-clad banks of Clyde.
Near the old bridge, so grim and gray,
A small, devoted army lay
An army sworn to fight till death,
For Gospel, Covenant, and Faith—
Christians undaunted, calm, and brave.
Who sought for freedom--or a *grave!*
And soon they saw the foe advancing,
The sunbeams on their weapons glancing
Advancing swift, with steady tread,
By ruthless, stern commanders led—
By Claver'se, Monmouth, and Dalzell—
The worshippers of God to quell.
The Covenanters God invoke
To save them from th' oppressor's yoke.
And soon from bank to bank there rang
The sound of strife, the battle's clang:
And all the ranks, in fierce commotion,
Swayed like the storm-driv'n waves of ocean—
And many a hero gasps for breath,
Then falls into the arms of death;
Above the noise and din of strife
Rise oaths, and yells, and cries for life;
And soon o'erwhelmed by that vast sea.
The Covenanters have to flee.
Fast o'er the bridge the victors crowd,
And bloody Claver'se shouts aloud—
" No prisoners take, nor mercy show;
Haste, haste! and kill each flying foe!"

The river's banks are covered o'er
With victims weltering in their gore—
Some wounded, dying, many dead—
O'er all the field their weapons spread.
Right in the centre of the scene,
Where all the hottest fight had been,
Poor Robin Lambie's body lay,
A senseless, bleeding piece of clay—
His body, yes; but ah! his soul
Had reached that wished-for, higher goal—
Had joined the ransomed, white arrayed,
Who, e'en when sun and stars shall fade,
Shall shine, sweet jewels of renown,
Immortal, lustrous, in God's crown.

All nature long had sunk to rest,
The birds asleep within each nest;
The moon her pale beams downward threw,
Giving to earth a ghostly hue;
O'er all the earth was heard no sound,
Stern silence reigned o'er all around.
Beside where Robin Lambie lay,
A pulseless, sightless piece of clay,
With blood-drops 'mong his yellow hair,
A female form knelt in despair;
'Twas faithful loving Mary Rae,
Who wiped the clotted blood away,—
Whose dreams so preyed upon her mind
That she had left her home behind,
Following the army from afar,
Undaunted by the din of war,

Had roamed the field of battle over
Until she found her martyr'd lover ;
Then down she knelt, so young, so fair,
Her heart nigh bursting with despair—
The tear-drops raining down her cheek ;
But ah ! no one can deem her weak.
Soon passed her sad, despairing mood,
Then stern and resolute she stood,
Dashed from her eye the burning tear
And mourned no more his sad career.
The lifeless body, stained with gore,
With superhuman strength she bore
Far from the dreadful battle scene
To where a fountain flows serene—
A pleasant, little rippling rill,
Within the lea-lands of Brownhill—
Then, fainting with her heart's great grief,
Her burdened spirit found relief.

.　　.　　.　　.　　.

Unto this day there may be seen,
Within a circle bright and green,
A little stone-protected mound—
'Twas here the faithful pair were found ;
And often travellers pause awhile
Beside the little rustic style
Which guards the grave of Mary Rae
And he who fell on that sad day.

www.ingramcontent.com/pod-product-compliance
Lightning Source LLC
Chambersburg PA
CBHW020621030726
47497CB00007B/2358